Contents

CHAPTER ONE

THE BITTER AWAKENING

The air in the monastery was deathly still, as if the ancient walls themselves were holding their breath, waiting. The wind that had once howled through the cracks in the stone was gone, leaving only the faint echo of Silas's final, desperate cry hanging in the air. His body had crumpled to the cold stone floor, limp and lifeless, as the blackness swallowed him whole.

Isabelle's voice rang out in the silence, sharp with panic. "Silas! Silas, no!" Her hands, trembling, reached for him as Helena's words hung heavy in the room, a warning that still echoed in her mind.

The vial had fallen from Silas's grasp, rolling across the floor with a hollow clink as everything went still. For a long moment, no one moved. The darkness seemed to wrap around them all, oppressive and unrelenting.

And then, slowly, he stirred.

Silas's eyes opened, but they were not the clear, human eyes of a man who had been freed from centuries of torment. They were the same ice-blue, piercing eyes that had seen countless deaths, countless nights, still glowing faintly with the eerie light of the vampire within.

The realization hit him like a fist to the gut. He was still a vampire.

Silas sat up slowly, his hand pressed to his chest as if trying to feel for something some sign of mortality, some spark of the human life he had longed for. But there was nothing. His body was still cold, the hollow emptiness still echoing in his heart. His skin, pale and unyielding, gave no warmth. His senses sharpened to a supernatural edge still picked up the faintest rustle of fabric, the softest whisper of wind through the stones.

He hadn't changed. He was still a creature of the night.

The crushing weight of disappointment settled in his chest like lead, squeezing the breath from his lungs. Silas ran a hand through his dark hair, tugging at the strands in frustration as he knelt on the ground. His heart or whatever was left of it felt as though it had shattered into pieces.

It didn't work.

He had risked everything, taken the potion with a sliver of hope that he might break free from the curse that had bound him for so long. But now, as the reality settled in, it felt like a cruel joke. He was still the monster he had always been.

His thoughts swirled in a chaotic storm, a mixture of anger, sorrow, and disbelief. Why? Why couldn't I be free?

The silence was broken by the sound of soft footsteps. Isabelle knelt beside him, her face etched with concern, her sapphire eyes filled with love and sorrow. Her hands reached for his, gently pulling him close. "Silas," she whispered, her voice trembling. "It's going to be okay..."

He shook his head, his jaw tightening as his chest tightened with bitter frustration. "It's not okay, Isabelle. It didn't work. I'm still this... this thing. I'm still a monster." His voice was raw, his anger barely contained. He couldn't look at her, not with the weight of his failure bearing down on him. He had promised her a life, a future where he could walk beside her as a man, not a cursed creature bound to the darkness.

Isabelle's grip tightened on his hand, her gaze softening with compassion. "You're not a monster," she whispered fiercely. "You're Silas. The man I love. That's all that matters."

Her words, full of warmth and love, should have soothed him, but instead, they tore at him. How could she still love him, still see him as anything more than the cursed being he was? He had wanted to be more for her to give her a life free from the shadow of the curse, free from the hunger that constantly clawed at him. But now, he couldn't. The thought of eternity stretched out before him again, a never-ending road of loneliness and blood.

He turned his head away, staring at the cold stone floor. "I wanted to be human again. For you." His voice was barely more than a whisper, thick with the weight of his disappointment.

Isabelle leaned closer, her hands cupping his face, gently pulling him to meet her gaze. "You are enough, Silas. You've always been enough. I don't care what you are, vampire or human. I love you, and that's never going to change."

Her words cut through the darkness that threatened to swallow him whole. Her love was there, unwavering, despite everything. And yet, the gnawing ache of disappointment wouldn't leave him. He had wanted this not just for her, but for himself. He had wanted to shed the curse that had weighed him down for centuries, to feel life again, to grow old. To escape the constant, relentless hunger.

Helena, who had been standing at a respectful distance, stepped closer, her eyes filled with a quiet wisdom. "Silas," she said gently, "perhaps this was never meant to change you in the way you hoped."

Silas frowned, turning his attention to her, frustration simmering beneath the surface. "What do you mean?"

Helena looked at him with a mixture of pity and understanding. "The curse... the power you carry... maybe it isn't something that can be erased. Maybe it's not your fate to return to what you were. Maybe you're meant for something greater."

Her words hung in the air, thick with meaning. Silas felt the weight of them press against his already burdened soul. Something greater? He hadn't wanted greatness. He had wanted to be free. He had wanted peace, a chance to live as he once had without the darkness, without the hunger.

"I don't want power," Silas said quietly, his voice barely a whisper. "I wanted to be human. I wanted..." He faltered, unable to finish the sentence. He wanted a life, a future, something real something more than the endless night.

Helena stepped closer; her eyes soft but resolute. "Perhaps you were never meant to be human again. Perhaps this course, this power, is something you must learn to wield. Not as a curse, but as a force for good."

Silas closed his eyes, her words swirling in his mind like a storm. Was it possible? Was his curse not something to escape, but something to embrace? The thought sent a chill through him. He didn't know if he was strong enough for that, didn't know if he could bear the weight of eternity again.

Isabelle's hand on his arm brought him back to the present. Her touch was gentle, grounding him in the moment, pulling him out of the spiral of his thoughts. "Whatever happens, we face it together," she said softly, her voice filled with quiet determination. "You don't have to do this alone."

Silas opened his eyes, gazing at her with a mixture of love and sorrow. How had he been so fortunate to find her? To have her love, even now, even after everything? His heart ached with gratitude and grief, knowing that he could never fully repay the depth of her devotion.

The wind outside the monastery picked up again, rattling the ancient windows and sending a low howl through the room. The atmosphere was thick with tension, the weight of the past and the future pressing down on them. But as Silas stood, pulling Isabelle to her feet with him, he felt a new resolve settle in his chest.

Maybe Helena was right. Maybe he wasn't meant to be human again. Maybe his fate was something else, something greater.

But whatever it was, he would face it. For Isabelle. For himself.

"I'll figure it out," he said quietly, his voice filled with a newfound determination. "I don't know what's coming, but I'll figure it out."

Helena nodded, her expression calm but serious. "There's much more to uncover, Silas. We've only just begun."

And as the wind howled through the ancient stone halls, Silas knew that their journey was far from over. He had not become human again, but perhaps there was more to his curse than he had ever realized. The path ahead was uncertain, full of danger and darkness, but for the first time in centuries, he felt a flicker of hope.

It wasn't over. Not yet.

But in the silence of the monastery, something darker stirred. Something ancient and watching, biding its time. Silas could feel it, just beyond the edge of his awareness. The fight wasn't over this was only the beginning.

And the darkness wasn't done with him yet.

Chapter Two

Shadows in the Night

The night outside the monastery was heavy with tension, as if the world itself held its breath, waiting for something to happen. The ancient stone walls were silent now, but Silas could still feel the weight of the monastery's secrets pressing down on him. Something deeper lurked here, something older than even the curse that had bound him for centuries. He could feel it, a dark presence that had been watching them all along, silent and still, as though it had been observing, learning. It was a creature of the night, just like him, but ancient... more ancient than anything he had ever encountered.

Helena was packing away the remnants of the ritual, her face drawn in concentration as she tied up the vials and the text they had used. Isabelle stood beside Silas, her hand resting lightly on his arm, her eyes fixed on him with concern. Silas could feel her warmth against his skin, but even that wasn't enough to shake the feeling that something was wrong.

It wasn't just his failure to become human again. It wasn't just the crushing disappointment that sat like a stone in his chest. No, it was something else. The presence that had been lingering just outside the edges of his awareness, watching... waiting.

Silas's eyes narrowed as he scanned the dark corners of the room, his heightened senses picking up the faintest shift in the air. For a moment, he thought he saw a shadow move—an unnatural movement, too deliberate to be the wind or the flicker of torchlight. His muscles tensed, instinct taking over. There was something else here.

And then, just as suddenly as it had appeared, the presence vanished. The shadow that had been watching them slipped away, retreating into the night without a trace, like a predator that had decided its prey wasn't worth the effort yet. Silas's eyes flickered, searching the darkness, but the creature, whatever it had been, was gone.

A chill ran down his spine.

"What is it?" Isabelle asked, her voice soft but concerned. She could sense the shift in his energy, the tension that rippled through his body like a bowstring pulled taut.

Silas shook his head, though his gaze remained fixed on the shadows. "There was something here," he murmured, his voice low. "Something ancient like the creature we just killed."

Helena paused, glancing up from her work, her brow furrowed. "I didn't sense anything," she said cautiously, though there was a flicker of worry in her eyes. "What kind of presence?"

Silas's eyes flicked toward her. "It wasn't human," he replied, his voice strained with unease. "And it wasn't like Lucian. It was something else. Older. Stronger." He paused, swallowing the lingering dread that clawed at him. "But it didn't attack. It was just... watching."

A heavy silence fell over the room, the weight of Silas's words settling over them like a shroud. Isabelle's grip on his arm tightened, and Helena's expression grew more guarded.

"Do you think it was part of the curse?" Isabelle asked quietly, her voice trembling with worry. "Something... tied to it?"

Silas shook his head, his jaw tightening. "I don't know," he admitted, his voice laced with frustration. "But whatever it was, it's not something I've encountered before."

And that unsettled him more than he wanted to admit. He had lived through centuries of darkness, fought monsters and demons that had stalked the night. But this... this was something else. Something that felt more like an ancient god than a mere vampire.

Helena stepped forward, her eyes narrowing thoughtfully. "If it's ancient, it may be tied to the origin of the curse," she suggested, her voice quiet but certain. "The monastery is filled with old magic, old energies. It could be something that's been here for centuries, guarding the secrets that this place holds."

Silas clenched his fists, his heart still racing. "Or it could be something worse," he muttered darkly, his mind racing with possibilities.

But there was no time to dwell on it now. The presence, whatever it had been, was gone. And they needed to return to New York. Silas glanced at Isabelle, her face pale and drawn from the stress of everything they had just endured. They couldn't stay here any longer.

"Let's get out of here," he said, his voice firm. "We can figure the rest out later."

The journey back to New York was long and exhausting, each step of the way filled with uncertainty. Silas couldn't shake the lingering dread of the creature that had been watching them. It stayed with him, gnawing at the edges of his mind like a persistent shadow. He felt as if it was still there, hiding in the periphery of his vision, waiting for the right moment to strike.

Isabelle remained at his side, her presence a comforting balm against the storm of emotions swirling inside him. She was quiet, but her hand in his was a constant reminder of what he was fighting for. Her love had saved him from despair more times than he could count, but now, in the wake of his failure to turn human again, Silas wondered if he could truly protect her from the darkness that was closing in around them.

Helena had arranged their passage back to New York discreetly, and they traveled under the cover of night, avoiding attention. The journey from the outskirts of Budapest to the heart of the city was uneventful, though Silas couldn't shake the feeling of being watched. Every dark alley, every fleeting shadow felt like the eyes of the ancient creature he had sensed in the monastery. But nothing revealed itself.

Their passage took them by train through the heart of Europe, the sprawling cities and countryside blurring together as they made their way west. The quiet rhythm of the train provided little comfort for Silas, whose mind was still reeling from the events at the monastery.

On their third night of travel, they arrived in Paris, a city that Silas knew well. It was a place filled with ghosts from his past, memories of a time when he had still been struggling to accept his fate. The streets of Paris held both beauty and tragedy for him, and he couldn't help but feel a pang of nostalgia as they moved through the dimly lit avenues.

But Paris was not the city it once was. It had changed, just as Silas had. The once-bustling streets were now quieter, the energy of the city dulled by modernity and time. As they passed through the narrow streets, they encountered few people just the occasional figure drifting through the fog-draped night.

One such figure caught Silas's attention. A man, tall and lean, dressed in dark clothing, with eyes that gleamed in the moonlight. He was standing on the corner of a narrow street, his gaze fixed on them as they passed. There was something unsettling about him, something that set Silas on edge.

Helena noticed it too. She leaned closer to Silas, her voice barely above a whisper. "That man... he's been following us since we arrived."

Silas's eyes narrowed, his body tensing. He had sensed something off the moment they stepped foot in Paris, but now it was clear someone, or something, was watching them. He turned his gaze toward the man, his supernatural senses picking up the faintest hint of dark energy radiating from him.

The man smiled a slow, unsettling smile and then disappeared into the shadows.

"He's not human," Silas muttered, his fists clenching. "He's something else."

Isabelle's face grew pale, her eyes wide with worry. "Who is he? What does he want?"

Helena shook her head, her brow furrowed. "I don't know. But we need to be careful."

Their journey through Paris was brief, but the encounter with the mysterious figure left Silas on edge. By the time they arrived at the port for their passage across the Atlantic, he was even more convinced that they were being followed.

The ocean voyage was uneventful, the rocking of the ship and the endless expanse of water providing a brief respite from the constant tension. But even then, Silas couldn't fully relax. His mind was still occupied with the creature from the monastery, and the man in Paris, both shadows, both watching.

When they finally arrived in New York, the city greeted them with its usual chaotic energy. The streets were crowded, the noise and bustle of life filling the air with a constant hum. But to Silas, it felt different. The city, once his home, now felt foreign its bright lights and busy streets a sharp contrast to the quiet, ancient world they had just left behind.

As they stepped off the ship and made their way through the streets, Silas felt the weight of the journey settling over him. He hadn't found the freedom he had sought. He hadn't become human again. And now, with the presence of an ancient creature haunting his thoughts, he knew that the darkness in his life was far from over.

As they made their way back to the safe haven of Silas's mansion, Helena's words echoed in his mind. "Maybe you were destined for something greater."

But what? What could be greater than the simple life he had wanted with Isabelle? What could possibly lie ahead that was worth the weight of immortality, the endless hunger, and the constant battle against the night?

He didn't know the answer. But whatever it was, he knew that the ancient creature was still out there, watching, waiting.

And so, as the streets of New York welcomed them home, Silas couldn't shake the feeling that something far darker was on the horizon.

Chapter Three

Love and Shadows

New York City never truly slept. The city thrummed with life its pulse beating through the neon lights and the bustling streets, even as the night stretched into the small hours of the morning. But for Silas, the noise faded into the background as he stood by the large window of his mansion, overlooking the glittering skyline. His thoughts were far from the city's hum of activity. Instead, they were consumed by the warmth of Isabelle's presence beside him and the dark shadows that lingered in the corners of his mind.

The mansion was quiet, a sharp contrast to the busy streets below. Inside its walls, everything felt frozen in time elegant, yet cold. The heavy drapes, the grand marble staircase, the high ceilings, all remnants of a past he could never fully leave behind. Yet, even in this place of stillness and old memories, something had shifted. Isabelle's love, her gentle presence, had brought a light into his world that he had thought long extinguished.

He looked down at her now, sitting in one of the leather armchairs by the fireplace, her hair glowing in the soft light, her sapphire eyes fixed on the flickering flames. She was lost in thought, as if she too was trying to make sense of everything that had happened. Silas's heart swelled with gratitude. She had chosen him despite the curse, despite the darkness that followed him like a shadow.

He didn't deserve her. But now that she was here, he couldn't imagine his life without her.

The fire crackled softly, casting flickering shadows across the walls. Silas's gaze shifted to Helena, who sat across from Isabelle, flipping through an old book of ancient texts. Her brow was furrowed in concentration, the dim light casting long shadows over her sharp features. She had been a constant presence throughout this journey a true friend, someone who had guided him and offered her unwavering support.

Silas had lived for centuries, but friendship had never come easily. He had kept people at arm's length for so long, isolating himself in the prison of his immortality. But Helena had broken through that, her knowledge and determination offering him hope when he had thought all was lost. She had fought beside him, risked everything to help him break the curse, even if it hadn't worked. Her loyalty was something he cherished more than he could put into words.

He stepped away from the window, moving toward the fire where the two women sat. His boots were silent on the polished wood floor, his movements graceful, almost predatory, but his expression was soft. He was trying to adjust to the life he had now, this new existence filled with both love and lingering shadows.

As he sat beside Isabelle, she leaned into him, resting her head against his shoulder. Her touch was soft, comforting. For a moment, Silas allowed himself to simply exist in the warmth of her presence, feeling the steady beat of her heart and the soft rise and fall of her chest.

"I'm so lucky to have you," he whispered, his voice barely audible over the crackling of the fire.

Isabelle smiled softly, her eyes still on the flames. "I'm the lucky one, Silas. I wouldn't be here without you."

Silas shook his head slightly, a pang of guilt settling in his chest. "I don't deserve you. Not after everything I've done... after what I've become."

Isabelle lifted her head, her sapphire eyes meeting his. "You are not a monster, Silas. I've told you before, and I'll keep telling you until you believe it. You saved me. You've saved so many people, even if you can't see it." Her hand gently cupped his face, her touch sending a wave of warmth through him. "I love you, Silas. No matter what you are, I love you."

His heart clenched, the weight of her words settling deep within him. Her love was a gift one that he had never thought he would be worthy of, especially after centuries of living in the darkness. But here she was, offering him a second chance at the love he had lost so long ago.

Silas pulled her closer, his arms wrapping around her as if he could shield her from the world. The scent of her hair, the feel of her body against his, it was all so fragile, so precious. And he was grateful. Grateful for her love, for this moment, for this second chance at happiness that he had thought impossible.

But beneath that gratitude, beneath the warmth of her love, there was something else, something darker. A nagging sense of unease that wouldn't let him rest. The creature that had watched them from the shadows in the monastery... it hadn't attacked. It hadn't done anything at all. It had simply observed. And that, more than anything, terrified Silas.

Why had it remained hidden? What had it been waiting for?

Helena's voice broke the silence, drawing Silas's attention. "You're still thinking about the creature, aren't you?" she asked, her gaze lifting from the pages of the book she had been studying.

Silas nodded, his grip on Isabelle tightening slightly. "Yes. It was powerful. Older than anything I've encountered before. I don't understand why it didn't attack us."

Helena closed the book gently, her fingers running over the worn leather cover. "Ancient beings like that don't operate on the same principles as we do. It may have been observing us, waiting for something. Or perhaps it was testing us."

"Testing us for what?" Isabelle asked, her voice filled with concern. "If it wanted to attack, why didn't it?"

"That's what worries me," Silas muttered, his jaw tightening. "If it's as old and powerful as I think it is, then it doesn't need to rush. It has time on its side. It can wait until the moment is right."

Helena nodded, her expression serious. "Whatever it is, we need to be prepared. There's more at play here than just Lucian's death or your failed transformation. The creature's presence means something, and we need to find out what."

Silas's thoughts churned, the weight of the situation pressing down on him. The creature had been there, watching him, and now it was out there somewhere, waiting for the right moment to strike. But why? And what did it want?

His gaze drifted back to the window, where the city lights flickered in the distance. Despite everything despite Isabelle's love, despite having Helena by his side, there was a deep, gnawing fear in his gut. The creature had not shown itself fully, and that terrified him. It was waiting for something. But what?

His surroundings felt both familiar and foreign. The grand mansion, with its sweeping staircases and rooms filled with relics from centuries past, had always been a place of solitude for him. But now, it felt like a fortress on the verge of being breached, the shadows outside creeping closer with every passing night. The quiet elegance of the rooms, the soft flickering of candles it all felt fragile, as if it could be shattered by the slightest push from the darkness.

"I don't want to lose this," Silas said quietly, his eyes fixed on the city beyond the window. "I don't want to lose you."

Isabelle leaned into him, her hand resting on his chest. "You won't," she said softly. "We'll face whatever comes. Together."

Silas closed his eyes, savoring the warmth of her words, but the fear still gnawed at him. The creature from the monastery wasn't done with them. It had watched, it had waited, and it would return. Silas knew it in his bones. And when it did, they would have to be ready.

He just hoped they would be strong enough.

The days following their return to New York passed quietly, but there was a tension that lingered in the air, an unspoken fear that none of them could shake. Silas continued to keep a close watch on the city, his instincts sharper than ever, but there was no sign of the creature. It had disappeared, leaving only the memory of its presence in the monastery, and the cold dread that it would return.

In the meantime, life went on. Helena threw herself into research, poring over ancient texts in search of answers about the creature, the curse, and the unknown forces at play. Isabelle stayed close to Silas, offering him comfort and love, though he could see the worry in her eyes whenever she thought he wasn't looking.

And Silas... Silas remained vigilant. His heart, once hardened by centuries of loss and despair, now softened by love, still carried the weight of the unknown. But he had Isabelle. He had Helena. And for the first time in a long time, he wasn't alone.

But even love couldn't keep the shadows at bay forever.

Chapter Four

The Gathering Storm

The following days passed in a blur of routine and restless tension. The cold winds of winter had settled over New York, biting through the city streets, sending chills even into the ancient walls of Silas's mansion. The fireplaces roared in nearly every room, but despite the warmth of the flames, a deep unease settled over the house. Something was coming, Silas could feel it in his bones.

He sat in his study, gazing out of the frost-covered window at the city beyond. It was dusk, and the dying light cast a golden glow over the skyline. But even the beauty of the evening couldn't pull him from the storm brewing inside him. Isabelle had retired to the sitting room after dinner, her smile warm but tired, and Helena had secluded herself in the library, consumed by her research.

Something's coming. Silas couldn't shake the thought, the nagging sense of impending doom. The creature they had encountered in the monastery, its presence still hung over him like a spectre. He had encountered many dark things in his centuries, but this was different. This was older. More dangerous.

Silas stood abruptly, pacing the length of the room. His movements were graceful, silent, but the tension in his muscles was unmistakable. His mind raced as he turned the events of the past weeks over and over in his head. Why hadn't the creature attacked? Why had it been watching?

Just as his frustration reached its peak, there was a soft knock at the door. He turned, and there, standing in the doorway, was Isabelle. Her long brunette hair was loose around her shoulders, and she wore a soft expression of concern, her sapphire eyes watching him carefully.

"You're restless," she said, stepping into the room. She crossed the floor to stand beside him, her hand brushing his arm gently.

Silas let out a slow breath, feeling the tension in his chest loosen slightly just at her touch. "I can't stop thinking about it," he admitted, his voice low. "Whatever that thing was... it's out there. Waiting."

Isabelle's brow furrowed, and she took his hand in hers, squeezing it gently. "We'll face it, whatever it is," she said softly. "You don't have to carry this alone."

Silas looked down at her, his heart swelling with gratitude, but also fear. She had saved him, brought light back into his dark existence. But how long could he protect her from the shadows that seemed to close in on them?

What if I fail her?

He clenched his jaw, pushing the thought away, and pulled her close, wrapping his arms around her. Isabelle leaned into him, her warmth grounding him, but the darkness still lingered in the back of his mind.

As they stood together, enveloped in the quiet of the room, there was a sudden knock at the front door. The sharp sound echoed through the mansion, breaking the peace. Silas's senses immediately sharpened, his body tensing as he pulled away from Isabelle.

"What now?" Isabelle whispered; her eyes wide with concern.

Silas didn't respond, his attention already focused on the unfamiliar presence beyond the door. Whoever or whatever it was, it wasn't human. He could feel the faint pulse of dark energy radiating from the entryway. His jaw tightened, and he moved swiftly toward the front hall, Isabelle close behind him.

When he reached the door, Helena was already there, her hand hovering over the knob, her face tense with anticipation. She glanced back at Silas, her eyes questioning. "It's not one of ours," she murmured.

Silas gave a curt nod, his hand moving to grip the cold metal knob. He pulled the door open slowly, ready for whatever awaited them on the other side.

Standing in the doorway was a man. He was tall, lean, with sharp features that seemed almost too perfect, too symmetrical. His skin was pale, but there was a sheen of unnatural beauty about him, the kind that only came from centuries of immortality. His dark hair was slicked back, and his eyes dark and intense, flicked over Silas and the others with an unreadable expression.

"Good evening," the man said smoothly, his voice carrying an eerie calm that made the hairs on the back of Silas's neck stand on end. "I hope I'm not intruding."

"You're not welcome here," Silas growled, stepping forward slightly, his body positioned protectively between Isabelle and the stranger.

The man's lips curled into a thin smile, but there was no warmth in it. "My name is Ambrose," he said, ignoring Silas's hostility. "I believe we have much to discuss."

"I don't think so," Silas replied coldly, his eyes narrowing. He could sense the darkness within Ambrose, the power that pulsed beneath his composed exterior. He was a vampire, but there was something more something old and dangerous.

Ambrose chuckled softly, his eyes flicking to Isabelle before returning to Silas. "You've made quite the impression recently, haven't you, Silvanus De Vico? The death of Lucian... the attempted transformation... you've attracted attention."

Silas's chest tightened. The death of Lucian had sent ripples through the vampire world, but he hadn't expected it to bring someone like Ambrose to his doorstep. "I don't know who you think you are," Silas said, his voice a low growl. "But I'm not interested in whatever you're selling."

Ambrose's smile widened, but his eyes remained cold. "Oh, I'm not here to sell you anything, Silas. I'm here to offer a warning." He took a step closer, his gaze darkening. "There are forces at play now, forces older than you can imagine. You've stirred something... ancient. And it's watching."

A chill ran down Silas's spine. The creature from the monastery.

"You're not the only one with power," Ambrose continued, his voice smooth as silk. "And there are those who would see you fall."

Silas's mind raced. Who? Why? "What do you want?" he demanded, his fists clenching at his sides.

"I want you to understand what's coming," Ambrose replied, his voice dropping to a deadly whisper. "The creature you encountered it's only the beginning. There are others, older than you, older than Lucian, older than this world. And they're watching you."

Helena stepped forward; her eyes sharp with suspicion. "And what do you get out of this warning?" she asked, her voice cutting through the tension.

Ambrose's gaze flickered to her, and for a moment, a flicker of amusement crossed his face. "Let's just say I have a vested interest in keeping the balance of power... intact." He turned his gaze back to Silas. "You've disrupted things, and now the old ones are stirring."

Silas's chest tightened with dread, but he kept his expression unreadable. Old ones? He had heard whispers of ancient beings, creatures who predated even the earliest vampires, but he had never believed them to be more than myth. Until now.

"If they're coming for me," Silas said, his voice low and dangerous, "then let them come."

Ambrose's smile faded, his expression turning serious. "You may think you're ready, Silas, but you have no idea what you're dealing with. These creatures... they are not bound by the same rules as us. They are gods compared to us."

Silas's jaw clenched, his mind reeling from the weight of Ambrose's words. The creature in the monastery, the darkness that had been watching him it wasn't just a random occurrence. Something much bigger was at play, something ancient and powerful.

"Why are you telling me this?" Silas asked, his voice tight with suspicion.

"Because," Ambrose said, his eyes gleaming with dark intent, "you and I are not so different. And when the time comes... you'll need allies."

Before Silas could respond, Ambrose stepped back, his figure disappearing into the night as swiftly as he had come. The heavy silence that followed was oppressive, the weight of his warning lingering in the air like a storm on the horizon.

Helena was the first to break the silence. "What the hell was that about?"

Silas stared out into the darkened street, his mind swirling with a thousand thoughts. "I don't know," he murmured, his voice filled with uncertainty. "But I don't like it."

Isabelle moved closer to him, her hand resting on his arm, her expression filled with concern. "Do you think he's right? About what's coming?"

Silas's chest tightened. He didn't want to admit it, but deep down, he knew Ambrose was right. The creature they had encountered in the monastery wasn't an isolated incident. Something far older was stirring, and they were in the center of it.

"I don't know," he said softly, his voice laced with dread. "But whatever's coming... we need to be ready."

Chapter Five

The Stranger's Secrets

The cold night air clung to the mansion, wrapping around its ancient walls like an embrace from the shadows themselves. Silas stood in the foyer, staring out the open door where Ambrose had disappeared into the dark streets of New York. The lingering chill of his presence was like a thorn in Silas's mind, a reminder of the growing unease that had settled over his world since the events in the monastery.

Ambrose.

The name alone left a bitter taste on Silas's tongue. He had encountered many vampires over the centuries, some ruthless, others lost to the hunger and madness that accompanied immortality, but none quite like Ambrose. There was something in the man's gaze, something ancient and detached, as though he were not bound by the same limitations that kept most of their kind tethered to the mortal world.

Silas's thoughts churned as he closed the door, locking it behind him. The weight of Ambrose's words lingered: "There are forces at play now, forces older than you can imagine." The warning was clear, but the purpose behind it was not. Why had Ambrose come to him? Why the sudden interest in warning him about the ancient creatures stirring beneath the surface of their world?

Something's not right.

Isabelle, standing beside him, watched his face with concern. "Silas?" she whispered softly. "What are you thinking?"

Silas shook his head, his expression dark. "I don't trust him," he muttered, his voice laced with suspicion. "I've known enough vampires in my time to know when one has an agenda. Ambrose didn't come here out of kindness or concern."

Helena stepped forward, her arms crossed as she stood near the doorway. "Ambrose is dangerous," she agreed, her eyes narrowing. "I've heard whispers of him before. He's one of the oldest. And from what I've gathered, he's not interested in the fate of humanity or even his own kind. He's a player in a much larger game."

"Larger game?" Isabelle asked, frowning as she looked between them. "What do you mean?"

Silas let out a breath, his hands clenching at his sides as his mind raced back through the centuries. "There are some vampires, ancient ones, who think of themselves as gods. They've lived so long that they've forgotten what it means to be anything else. They see the world as theirs to control, to shape according to their will. I've avoided most of them, kept to myself. But Ambrose... he's one of them."

Helena nodded in agreement. "He's a manipulator. Someone who uses his power and influence to bend others to his will. I've heard stories about him, centuries-old tales of kingdoms falling, empires crumbling, and somehow, Ambrose always emerges untouched, unscathed, like a phantom."

Silas paced the floor, his boots echoing softly against the marble as his mind turned over Ambrose's appearance and words. "He didn't just come to warn me. He came because he wants something."

Isabelle's face grew pale, and she instinctively moved closer to Silas, her hand resting lightly on his arm. "What do you think it is?"

Silas shook his head. "I don't know yet. But whatever it is, it's not good."

Ambrose was not a name whispered lightly in the vampire world. He had walked the earth for millennia, predating most civilizations. Some claimed he had been born in ancient Egypt, others whispered that he had once been a king in Mesopotamia, his reign long since forgotten by human history. Wherever he came from, one thing was certain—Ambrose had lived through the rise and fall of empires, watching from the shadows, always present but never exposed.

He wasn't like Lucian, who thrived on power and control through brute force. Ambrose was subtle, weaving his influence through the fabric of society, manipulating those in power with a careful hand. It was said that wars had been fought, treaties signed, and kings dethroned all at the quiet behest of Ambrose.

But what unnerved Silas the most was Ambrose's detachment from the world around him. There was a coldness in his eyes, a dispassionate gaze that spoke of someone who no longer saw humans or even fellow vampires as equals. To Ambrose, everything was a tool to be used, a means to an end. Silas had encountered vampires like him before—ancient beings who had lived so long that their sense of morality, of empathy, had eroded away. But Ambrose was different. He wasn't just old; he was calculating, patient, like a predator biding its time.

Silas had always mistrusted his own kind, for good reason. The vampire world was fraught with deception, betrayal, and greed. He had kept his distance from others for centuries, avoiding their politics, their power struggles, and their thirst for domination. His mistrust ran deep, stemming from the moment he had been turned—an act of betrayal that had severed his ties to humanity and bound him to an existence he had never wanted.

The thought of his own transformation, the curse that had been thrust upon him so many years ago, made his jaw tighten. He had been betrayed by those he once called friends, and since then, he had refused to allow himself to be used again. Ambrose, with all his charm and subtle manipulation, reminded Silas too much of that betrayal.

Something about him isn't right. Silas couldn't shake the feeling. Ambrose hadn't come to him by chance. The creature in the monastery, the warning about ancient forces stirring—it was all connected. But to what end?

Helena, sensing Silas's growing frustration, stepped forward. "We need to be careful," she said firmly. "Ambrose has a history of manipulating others, of setting events in motion that benefit him. If he's here, if he's watching you, it's because you're part of something bigger than you realize."

Silas nodded, his gaze still distant. "I know. But I don't like it."

That night, as the hours slipped away, Silas found himself alone in the darkened study once again, lost in thought. The fire had died down to embers, casting a faint orange glow over the room. His mind was a storm of conflicting emotions—gratitude for the love he had found with Isabelle, the steady presence of Helena by his side, and the unshakable dread that had settled in his gut since Ambrose's appearance.

Something bigger is coming.

The creature in the monastery... Ambrose's cryptic warning... the old ones stirring. It felt like the calm before a storm—one that would sweep away everything in its path.

Silas closed his eyes, leaning his head against the back of the chair. He had lived for so long, survived countless battles, betrayals, and heartbreaks. He had grown used to the constant pull of darkness, the weight of his own curse. But now, as he sat there in the quiet of the mansion, with Isabelle and Helena nearby, he realized that he had something to lose.

What if I can't protect them? What if this is bigger than me? The thought gnawed at him, filling him with a sense of helplessness that he hadn't felt in centuries. Isabelle had saved him from his own despair, pulled him out of the abyss he had been drowning in for so long. And Helena had become more than just an ally—she had become a true friend, someone he could trust.

But if Ambrose was right, if the old ones were stirring... he didn't know if he had the strength to face them.

And if I fall, what happens to them?

The mansion felt too quiet, too still, as if it too was waiting for something to happen. The shadows seemed to stretch longer in the corners of the room, and the silence was heavy, pressing down on him like a weight. Silas ran a hand through his dark hair, his mind racing. The thought of losing Isabelle, of losing Helena, was unbearable. He couldn't let that happen. Not again.

Hours later, just before dawn, Silas heard a soft knock at the door. He didn't need to turn to know it was Helena.

"You're still up," she said softly as she stepped into the room, her long coat wrapped around her. The fire's dying embers reflected in her eyes as she crossed the floor to stand beside him.

Silas nodded, his gaze still distant. "I can't sleep," he admitted.

Helena sat across from him, her eyes studying his face carefully. "Ambrose is in your head," she said gently, her voice filled with understanding. "But you can't let him control the way you move forward."

Silas let out a slow breath, his shoulders sagging slightly. "It's not just Ambrose. It's everything. The creature in the monastery, this talk of old forces... I don't know if I'm ready for what's coming."

Helena leaned forward, her expression serious but compassionate. "You don't have to be ready for everything. You just have to be ready to fight when the time comes. And you're not alone, Silas. You have us. You have Isabelle."

Silas looked up at her, his blue eyes filled with a mixture of gratitude and sorrow. "I'm not used to this," he confessed quietly. "I'm not used to having people who care about me... people I care about."

Helena smiled softly, her hand resting lightly on his. "Then you're just going to have to get used to it."

For the first time that night, Silas felt a faint glimmer of hope. He wasn't alone. And whatever storm was coming, they would face it together.

But even as the dawn's light began to creep through the window, casting the first rays of morning over the city, Silas couldn't shake the feeling that Ambrose was still watching, waiting in the shadows for the moment to strike.

CHAPTER SIX

ECHOES OF THE PAST

The early morning light filtered through the heavy curtains of the mansion, casting long, soft beams across the dark wood floors and illuminating the remnants of the night's tension. Silas sat in the study, staring at the faint glow that crept over the horizon. The city outside was slowly awakening, but inside these walls, the air was thick with the weight of unspoken thoughts and uncertain futures.

The confrontation with Ambrose still echoed in Silas's mind, playing over and over again like a warning he couldn't shake. The smoothness of Ambrose's voice, the chilling calm in his eyes, and the cryptic message about the ancient forces stirred something deep within Silas an instinct that had kept him alive for centuries but now left him more anxious than ever.

Something's coming. And I don't know how to stop it.

Silas clenched his jaw, his fingers tapping absently on the armrest of his chair as his mind raced. He wasn't afraid of battle, wasn't afraid of death. He had faced both too many times to count. But this was different. This wasn't a fight against a single enemy like Lucian or even another vampire. It was something older, something he didn't fully understand. And that terrified him more than he wanted to admit.

Isabelle, sitting across from him, sensed his turmoil. Her sapphire eyes watched him carefully, and though she didn't say anything, Silas could feel her concern radiating from her. She always seemed to know when he was lost in his thoughts, drifting into the darkness of his own mind. It had been that way since they had returned from the monastery. The distance between them wasn't physical….it was in his silence, his guarded expression, his quiet worry.

She wanted to help him, but didn't know how. And that pained her deeply.

He's shutting me out again. Isabelle's heart clenched as she watched Silas, his sharp features shadowed by the morning light. He had always been a mystery, even when they were together centuries ago. But now, after everything they had been through, she felt him pulling away, retreating into the safety of his solitude. She knew he was trying to protect her, but it only made her feel more helpless.

Is he ever going to let me in fully?

Her thoughts drifted back to the night in the monastery, to the moment she thought she had lost him forever. She had felt his heart stop, watched him fall to the ground, and in that moment, her own world had collapsed. The love she felt for him was deeper than anything she had ever known, stronger than the pull of time itself. And now that they were together again, all she wanted was to stand by his side to face whatever darkness was coming together.

But how could she help when he wouldn't open up to her? When he carried the weight of centuries alone?

Isabelle shifted in her seat, her fingers tracing the edge of the armrest as she tried to find the words. "Silas," she began softly, her voice breaking the silence, "you don't have to carry this burden by yourself."

Silas's gaze flickered toward her, his expression softening slightly. He knew she was right, knew that he was doing the very thing he had promised himself he wouldn't do. He had vowed not to shut her out, to let her be a part of his world, his fight. But old habits die hard, and Silas had spent too many years living in isolation, convinced that allowing anyone too close would only bring them harm.

"I'm not trying to shut you out," he said quietly, his voice rough with emotion. "I just don't know how to protect you from this... from what's coming."

Isabelle stood and crossed the room, settling beside him. She gently took his hand, her fingers warm against his cool skin. "You don't have to protect me from everything. I'm not the same person I was centuries ago, Silas. I'm stronger now. We face this together, remember?"

Silas's chest tightened at her words. Her love, her unwavering faith in him, was something he didn't feel he deserved. But it was also the one thing that kept him anchored to this world. He looked into her eyes, seeing the determination there the strength she had gained over the years.

"I don't want to lose you," he whispered, his voice barely audible.

"You won't," Isabelle replied softly. "But you have to let me help."

In another part of the mansion, Helena sat in the grand library, surrounded by towering bookshelves that stretched from floor to ceiling, filled with tomes older than most of the world's nations. The room was dim, save for the soft glow of a single lamp that cast its warm light over the ancient texts spread across the large wooden table in front of her. The silence of the library was comforting, but her mind was anything but calm.

She had spent the past several hours poring over Silas's vast collection of books, searching for any reference to the creature they had encountered in the monastery. The old ones. The ancient forces Ambrose had spoken of. The more she read, the more she realized just how little they knew about what they were up against.

How do you fight something that's existed longer than recorded history?

Helena's fingers traced the worn edges of one of the books, her brow furrowed in concentration. She had always been fascinated by the occult, by the hidden histories of the world, but this was different. This wasn't academic curiosity this was a battle for survival. She had spent her life seeking knowledge, but now she felt the weight of her role more than ever.

Silas is relying on me.

That thought had been circling in her mind since Ambrose's warning. She had always been a scholar, an expert in vampire lore, but now she had to be more than that. She had to be their guide through the darkness that lay ahead. And the thought terrified her.

Her mind wandered back to the monastery, to the creature that had watched them from the shadows. It hadn't attacked. It hadn't even revealed itself fully. But its presence had been palpable, a force that seemed to ripple through the air like a storm waiting to break.

Why didn't it strike? What was it waiting for?

She flipped through another page, her eyes scanning the ancient symbols, the languages of long-dead civilizations. There had to be something here, some clue, some hint as to what they were dealing with. But the more she read, the more questions arose.

Helena leaned back in her chair, rubbing her temples as exhaustion crept in. She had been awake for too long, her mind swirling with possibilities, theories, and fears. But there was no time for rest. Whatever was coming, it was bigger than any of them had anticipated.

The door to the library creaked open, and Silas stepped inside, his expression unreadable as he crossed the room to stand beside her. Helena looked up from the book, offering him a tired smile.

"Any luck?" Silas asked quietly, his voice tinged with hope, though his eyes betrayed his doubt.

Helena shook her head. "Not yet. There are references to ancient creatures, beings that predate even the first vampires. But nothing concrete." She hesitated, her eyes scanning the pages in front of her. "It's like they exist in the spaces between history, whispers in forgotten languages. They're not just old, Silas. They're something else entirely."

Silas's jaw tightened as he absorbed her words. The thought of facing something older, something beyond their understanding, filled him with a sense of dread he hadn't felt in centuries. If they can't be killed, how can they be stopped?

"Keep looking," he said, his voice low but firm. "We need answers. Anything you can find."

Helena nodded, though the weight of the task ahead of her was beginning to settle heavily on her shoulders. "I'll keep searching. There has to be something here."

Silas's gaze lingered on her for a moment, gratitude flickering in his eyes. He didn't say it, but Helena could feel his appreciation for her efforts. She was more than just a scholar to him, now she was a trusted friend, someone he could rely on.

As Silas left the library, returning to the quiet of the study, his mind was a storm of conflicting emotions. He felt the weight of his responsibilities pressing down on him. He had spent centuries in isolation, disconnected from the world, but now everything felt so fragile. He had Isabelle's love, Helena's friendship two people he cared for deeply. And he couldn't bear the thought of losing either of them.

But how could he protect them when he didn't even know what he was up against?

The memories of the monastery, of Ambrose's warning, of the creature lurking in the shadows all swirled in his mind. The world felt as though it was on the brink of something terrible, something beyond his control. And for the first time in a long time, Silas felt powerless.

He stood by the window once more, gazing out at the city. The streets were still quiet, the early morning light casting a soft glow over the skyline. But beneath the calm, he could feel the storm coming. The darkness was growing, and it wouldn't be long before it reached them.

Isabelle appeared behind him, her presence a comforting warmth in the cold stillness of the room. She slipped her arms around his waist, resting her head against his back. "We'll figure this out, Silas," she whispered, her voice soft but strong. "We always do."

Silas closed his eyes, his hand covering hers as he let out a slow, steady breath. "I hope you're right," he whispered, though the doubt still lingered in his heart.

But even as he stood there, wrapped in Isabelle's embrace, his mind was elsewhere on the ancient forces stirring in the shadows, and the creature that had watched them from the dark, waiting for the moment to strike.

And in that moment, Silas knew one thing for certain: the fight was far from over.

CHAPTER SEVEN

WHISPERS OF THE PAST

The room was still, filled only with the gentle crackling of the fire and the soft breathing of Isabelle as she leaned against Silas. Her warmth grounded him, but inside his mind, a storm raged. The weight of Ambrose's visit, the lurking danger, and the fear of what was coming consumed his thoughts. Despite the quiet, Silas felt like he was teetering on the edge of something vast and terrible.

Something older. Something darker.

His instincts were screaming at him to act, but he didn't know how. He had no idea how to fight something ancient, something beyond even the oldest vampires he had ever known. Helena's research was ongoing, but the answers they needed remained elusive. It felt like they were grasping at shadows, trying to solve a puzzle without knowing what the pieces even looked like.

And then, like a bolt of lightning piercing through the fog of his thoughts, Silas remembered.

His body stiffened as the memory surged forward. A forgotten book. A book from long ago. Silas's mind raced, his heart pounding in his chest as the pieces fell into place.

The library. That old book in the city's public library.

It had been years, decades even, since he had last thought of it. He had been wandering the city late at night, restless and searching for distractions. The New York Public Library had been one of his sanctuaries a place to get lost in history, to drown out the endless noise of immortality with books.

One night, while roaming the dim, forgotten corners of the vast library, a single book had fallen from a shelf, as if pushed by unseen hands. It had tumbled onto the floor, its leather cover old and cracked, its pages yellowed and brittle with age. At first, Silas hadn't thought much of it just another artifact from a long-forgotten era. But when he had opened the book, the language inscribed on its pages had chilled him to his core.

It was written in a script he had only seen once before: Scritura Tenebris, the ancient language of the first vampires.

The memory hit Silas like a physical blow. He had spent hours poring over the pages, recognizing some of the symbols, but much of the text had been lost to time. It spoke of creatures older than vampires, beings that had existed before the first blood was spilled. It spoke of darkness primordial forces that could not be tamed or controlled.

And it spoke of a great awakening.

Silas felt his breath catch in his throat. The book. The answers were in that book all along.

How could he have forgotten?

Isabelle, sensing the shift in his body, pulled back slightly, her sapphire eyes filled with concern. "Silas? What is it?"

Silas stood abruptly, his mind racing. "There's a book," he muttered, his voice tight with urgency. "In the city's public library. It was hidden in the back, in one of the old wings. I found it years ago, but I never made the connection until now."

Helena, who had been deep in her research, looked up sharply at the mention of the book. "What kind of book?" she asked, her voice cautious but intrigued.

Silas's eyes darkened. "An old one. Older than most of the texts I've come across. It was written in Scritura Tenebris the language of the first vampires."

Helena's brow furrowed, her fingers stilling over the pages of her own book. "Scritura Tenebris? That language is nearly extinct. Very few have the knowledge to read it now."

Silas nodded, his expression grim. "I could only make out pieces of it, fragments here and there. But the parts I understood... it spoke of ancient creatures. Dark forces that existed before vampires. And it mentioned something about a great awakening."

"A great awakening?" Isabelle repeated, her voice barely above a whisper. "What does that mean?"

Silas shook his head. "I don't know. But if Ambrose is right, if these creatures are stirring, then it has to be connected. I should have paid more attention to that book. I should have—"

Helena interrupted him, her voice steady but intense. "It's not too late. If the book is still there, we can go back and study it properly. It might have the answers we need."

Silas's mind raced, a mixture of frustration and hope bubbling up inside him. The idea of going back to the library, of finding the book and delving into its secrets, filled him with both anticipation and dread. He knew that whatever was written in that ancient text could hold the key to stopping whatever was coming. But he also knew that it would not be easy.

Books like those texts filled with forbidden knowledge often carried their own dangers.

Later that night, they gathered in the mansion's grand hall, the weight of the decision pressing down on all of them. Silas paced the length of the room, his emotions swirling like the wind outside. He could feel the pull of the city, the need to go back to the library and find the book. But he also knew the risks.

"Do you really think it's still there?" Isabelle asked quietly, her voice filled with both hope and trepidation.

Silas stopped pacing and looked at her, his blue eyes flickering with uncertainty. "I don't know. But I have to try. If it's still there, it could give us the answers we need."

Helena stood by the fireplace, her arms crossed as she considered the situation. "If this book is as old as you say it is, it's possible someone else has already found it. Ambrose, or worse, one of the old ones."

Silas nodded, knowing full well that the book's presence in the library had always been precarious. It had been hidden in a section few ever visited, but that didn't mean it was safe. "I don't know who else could have found it. But it's the only lead we have."

A heavy silence fell over the room as they all considered the weight of the situation.

"We'll go tonight," Silas said finally, his voice filled with determination. "We can't afford to wait."

The New York Public Library stood like a sentinel in the night, its grand facade illuminated by the soft glow of streetlights. The building was quiet, the usual crowds long gone, leaving only the vast marble steps leading to the entrance. Silas, Isabelle, and Helena moved silently through the city streets, keeping to the shadows as they approached.

For most, the library was just another landmark, a place of learning and history. But to Silas, it was something more. It was a place of secrets, secrets buried beneath layers of time and dust. And tonight, those secrets might finally be revealed.

The three of them slipped through a side entrance, avoiding the main doors and the watchful eyes of any security that might be lingering inside. The library was vast, a labyrinth of bookshelves and forgotten rooms, but Silas remembered exactly where he had found the book all those years ago.

They made their way through the dimly lit corridors, their footsteps echoing softly off the polished floors. The air was thick with the smell of old paper and leather, the scent of time itself lingering in the air. Silas felt a strange sense of both nostalgia and dread as they passed through the familiar hallways.

It's still here. I know it is.

They reached the back of the library, where the oldest and most forgotten sections resided. Dust covered the shelves, and the air was thick with the weight of knowledge long since abandoned. Silas led them to a small alcove tucked away in a corner, hidden behind a row of towering bookshelves.

And there, on the bottom shelf, half-covered by dust and cobwebs, was the book.

It hadn't moved. It hadn't been touched.

Silas knelt, his fingers brushing against the cracked leather cover as a strange sense of relief and unease washed over him. The book was just as he remembered it, its dark cover worn with age, the edges of its pages brittle and yellowed. But the weight of the knowledge inside it, the power it held, was still as potent as ever.

He carefully opened the book, revealing the familiar script of Scritura Tenebris—the ancient language of the first vampires. The letters were sharp, angular, almost violent in their appearance. Silas could feel the magic, the darkness, pulsing from the pages as he ran his fingers over the symbols.

Helena knelt beside him, her eyes wide with awe. "This is it," she whispered, her voice filled with reverence. "This book... it's older than anything I've ever seen."

Silas nodded, his heart pounding in his chest. "It speaks of the old ones," he said quietly, his voice barely more than a whisper. "Of creatures that existed before vampires. Before the curse."

Helena's eyes flickered with understanding, her mind already piecing together the implications. "If the old ones are stirring, this might be the key to understanding why."

Silas flipped through the pages, recognizing fragments of the text he had seen before. But there were parts he hadn't fully understood them, symbols and phrases that seemed to shift and change before his eyes, as though the book itself was alive. As though it was hiding its true meaning from those who weren't ready to see.

Isabelle stood behind them, her hand resting on Silas's shoulder as she watched the scene unfold. The air around them seemed to hum with energy, and she couldn't shake the feeling that they were standing on the edge of something monumental. Something dangerous.

"What does it say?" Isabelle asked softly, her voice filled with a mixture of curiosity and fear.

Silas's eyes scanned the page, his heart racing as he read the ancient text. "It talks about the awakening of the old ones," he murmured. "That when the balance of power is disrupted, they will rise again. And when they do, they bring destruction with them."

Helena's face grew pale, her mind racing. "That must be what Ambrose was warning us about. The balance has been disrupted.... Lucian's death, the failed ritual. It's all connected."

Silas clenched his jaw, the weight of the revelation crashing down on him. The old ones were stirring. And they were coming.

But as he read further, something else caught his eye, a passage written in even darker ink, a phrase that sent a chill down his spine.

"The blood of the cursed shall be the key."

The words hung in the air like a death sentence, the weight of their meaning sinking into the room as the reality of the situation settled over them. The book, with all its ancient knowledge, had revealed the truth.

The old ones were coming. And Silas... Silas was the key.

Chapter Eight

Awakening the Forgotten

The words from the ancient text echoed in Silas's mind, as though the book itself was alive, speaking directly to him: "The blood of the cursed shall be the key." The weight of the sentence settled over him like a shroud, suffocating and cold. Silas could feel Isabelle's presence behind him, her soft breath close, but the distance between them felt vast. His heart hammered in his chest, not from the usual hunger or restlessness he had grown accustomed to as a vampire, but from something far worse: fear.

For the first time in centuries, Silas was truly afraid.

The ancient book lay open on the floor of the forgotten corner of the library, its cracked leather cover and brittle pages glowing dimly under the soft, ambient light. The letters, written in Scritura Tenebris, flickered like shadows across the page, alive with an energy that made Silas's skin crawl. This wasn't just an old book, it was a conduit, a vessel for something dark and powerful. Something that had been dormant for eons.

"The old ones," Silas whispered, his voice barely audible as his eyes scanned the page. Helena, kneeling beside him, peered over his shoulder, her face pale with concentration as she tried to decipher the script along with him.

"What does it say?" Isabelle asked, her voice trembling slightly.

Silas swallowed; his throat tight. "It talks about creatures... beings that existed before vampires, before humans. Primordial forces that have been asleep for millennia."

His heart sank as he read further, the words twisting in his mind like dark tendrils. The old ones were more than just ancient creatures, they were entities. Beings that had been worshiped as gods long before humans had walked the earth. They weren't bound by the rules of life and death. They were beyond that.

"They're not like us," Silas continued, his voice distant as his eyes flicked over the dark text. "They're... older. Stronger. They existed before the curse of vampirism. Before humans even knew how to fear the dark. They ruled the night, feeding on more than just blood...they consumed life itself. Destruction follows them wherever they go."

Helena's face grew paler with every word. "How many?" she asked, her voice tight.

Silas hesitated, his eyes scanning the page again, his mind struggling to process the enormity of what he was reading. "Seven," he finally answered, his voice barely above a whisper. "There are seven of them. Seven old ones. Each tied to a different aspect of life and death. They are the harbingers of the end."

The fear that had been gnawing at him since Ambrose's visit suddenly flared to life, sharp and immediate. Silas closed his eyes, trying to calm the storm that raged inside him. The thought of these beings awakening, of them rising to reclaim the world, filled him with a terror he hadn't felt since the day he had been turned.

They can't be stopped. Not by any of us.

The book described them in detail, but the descriptions felt more like nightmares than anything real. Each of the seven had a name, though the language of their names was too old to pronounce, too ancient to understand. But the images that came to Silas's mind were vivid terrifying. The first of the old ones, the one tied to decay and destruction, was said to take the form of a massive, shadowed beast. Its body was made of writhing black smoke, with glowing red eyes that pierced through the darkness. It fed on life itself, draining the world of energy, turning fertile lands into barren wastelands.

Another, bound to famine and drought, took the form of a towering skeletal figure, draped in a cloak of blackened, withered skin. It walked the earth and wherever it went, crops withered, rivers dried, and entire civilizations crumbled into dust.

The other five were equally horrifying, each representing a primal force of nature...death, madness, war, pestilence, and chaos. Together, they were a storm that could tear apart the fabric of the world itself.

They were gods once, before humans knew the names of gods. And they will be gods again when they awaken.

Silas's hands trembled as he closed the book, the weight of it too much to bear. He had fought many battles over the centuries seen death, war, and destruction. But this... this was different. This wasn't something he could fight with fangs and strength. This was an ancient force beyond anything he had ever encountered.

Isabelle knelt beside him, her hand resting on his arm. "Silas?" she whispered, her voice laced with worry. "What is it? What aren't you telling us?"

Silas couldn't meet her gaze. He couldn't tell her the truth. Not yet. He couldn't bear to see the fear in her eyes, the fear that he was feeling deep in his bones. Instead, he stood abruptly, turning away from both her and Helena as he tried to collect himself.

The blood of the cursed shall be the key.

Those words echoed in his mind again and again. The key. The blood of the cursed. His blood.

The truth hit him like a blow to the chest, and he felt his heart sink into a dark abyss. He was the key. His blood, the blood of a vampire was what would awaken the old ones. Somehow, he was tied to their awakening, bound to the ancient curse that had been woven into the fabric of time long before he was even born.

He closed his eyes, his fists clenching as the fear threatened to overwhelm him. How could I have missed this?

He had always thought of his curse as a personal burden something that had been forced upon him. But now, he realized it was much bigger than that. His curse, his immortality, was tied to something far darker. The old ones had been waiting for centuries, slumbering beneath the surface of reality, and now they were waking. And it was his blood that would open the door.

Helena's voice broke through his thoughts, her tone cautious but firm. "Silas, what aren't you telling us?"

Silas turned slowly, his eyes meeting Helena's and then Isabelle's. He could see the worry etched on their faces, the fear they were trying to keep at bay. He had been through so much with them fought beside them, trusted them with his life. But now, he didn't know if he could tell them the truth.

If they knew, they would see me differently. They would fear me.

But he couldn't keep it from them. Not when the danger was so close, not when their lives were at risk. They had a right to know, even if it meant losing the trust and love he had worked so hard to keep.

"I'm the key," he said finally, his voice tight with fear and regret. "My blood. It's what will wake them."

Isabelle's eyes widened, her hand flying to her mouth as the realization sank in. "What? How... how do you know?"

Silas held up the book, his hand shaking slightly. "It says it here. The blood of the cursed. My blood... it's tied to them. If they awaken, it'll be because of me."

Helena's face grew pale, her eyes narrowing in disbelief. "You're saying... that these creatures, these old ones... they need your blood to rise?"

Silas nodded, his heart heavy with guilt. "Yes. Somehow, my curse is connected to them. Maybe it's always been connected, and I just didn't see it until now."

A heavy silence fell over the room, the gravity of Silas's words sinking into the air like a lead weight. Isabelle stood frozen, her sapphire eyes filled with fear and sorrow as she struggled to process the truth.

"No," she whispered, shaking her head. "There has to be another way. This can't be the only answer."

Silas wished he could believe that. But the weight of the truth was undeniable. He had been cursed for centuries, and now, that curse had come full circle. It wasn't just about his immortality, it was about something much bigger, something that had been waiting for him all along.

"I don't know what we're supposed to do," Silas admitted, his voice cracking with emotion. "But if they're coming, we need to be ready."

Helena nodded slowly, her eyes dark with worry. "We need to find out more. There has to be something in these texts, something that can tell us how to stop this."

Isabelle's voice trembled as she spoke. "We'll figure it out. We have to."

But Silas wasn't so sure. As he stood there, the weight of his fate pressing down on him, he couldn't shake the fear that had taken root deep inside him. The old ones were stirring, and he was the key to their return.

What if I'm the one who destroys everything?

The night outside was darker than ever, the wind howling through the streets of New York like a warning. Inside the mansion, the air was thick with tension, the weight of the coming storm hanging over them all like a curse.

And in the distance, somewhere deep in the shadows of the city, something stirred. Something ancient. Something hungry.

Chapter Nine

The Weight of Destiny

The ancient book rested on the table in front of them, its cracked leather cover illuminated by the flickering candlelight. It seemed to pulse with its own dark energy, as though the words contained within were alive, waiting to unleash their secrets. Silas, Isabelle, and Helena sat around it in tense silence, each of them consumed by their own thoughts.

Silas stared at the open pages, his mind reeling from the revelation they had uncovered. The weight of what it meant pressed down on him like a vice, squeezing the air from his lungs. His blood, his very existence was the key to awakening the old ones. He had spent centuries trying to escape his curse, trying to live with it, and now he realized that it was never just about him. It was something far bigger, something woven into the fabric of time itself.

The questions churned in his mind, relentless and unyielding. Why me? Why my blood? What is it about my curse that ties me to these ancient beings?

He clenched his fists, his jaw tight with frustration. The book held so many answers, yet it also left him drowning in more questions. His immortality had always felt like a burden, a cruel twist of fate that kept him bound to the shadows. But now, it felt like something far more sinister like he had been marked, chosen for this terrible fate long before he had even been born.

His eyes scanned the ancient text, searching desperately for something, anything that could tell him how to stop this. How to fight back. But the more he read, the more hopeless it seemed. The book spoke of the old ones in cryptic terms, describing their immense power, their hunger, and the destruction they would bring when they awoke. But it offered no clues, no weaknesses, no hints about where they were hiding or how to defeat them.

If they even can be defeated.

Silas's heart sank further with every page they turned. He had hoped, naively perhaps, that the book would hold the key to stopping them. But all it seemed to offer were grim prophecies and vague warnings. The old ones were coming, and the world would burn when they did. That much was clear. What wasn't clear was how to stop them.

Helena leaned closer to the book, her fingers tracing the sharp, angular script of Scritura Tenebris. Her face was pale, her eyes narrowed in concentration as she studied the words, but Silas could tell by the way her hands trembled that she was just as unnerved as he was.

"This language," she murmured, her voice low. "It's older than anything I've seen. Even the oldest texts we've studied don't come close to this. These symbols... they shift, almost like they're alive."

Silas nodded, his eyes fixed on the page. He had noticed it too the way the symbols seemed to twist and shimmer, as if the book itself was trying to keep its secrets hidden. It was as if the knowledge within it was too dangerous, too ancient, for mortal minds to comprehend.

Isabelle, sitting beside him, glanced up from the book, her face etched with worry. "There has to be something here," she said, her voice filled with a desperate hope. "There has to be a way to stop them."

Silas's heart ached at the sound of her voice. He could see the fear in her eyes, the fear that matched his own. She was clinging to hope, but he wasn't sure if there was any left to hold on to.

"I don't know if there is," Silas admitted, his voice heavy with defeat. "These creatures... they're not like anything we've ever faced. They're older than vampires. Older than death itself. How do you fight something that existed before the world even knew how to die?"

His words hung in the air like a dark cloud, and the room seemed to grow colder, the candlelight flickering as if in response to the despair that settled over them. Silas's mind raced, a whirlwind of thoughts and emotions that he couldn't control. He had faced so much over the centuries fought battles, survived betrayals, endured the loneliness of immortality. But this... this was different. This was something he couldn't fight with brute strength or cunning. This was a force of nature, a storm that would sweep them all away.

Helena's voice broke through the silence, her tone cautious but determined. "There has to be a reason it's you, Silas. Your blood... your curse... it's tied to them. But why? There has to be something special about your bloodline, something that makes you different."

Silas shook his head, frustration gnawing at him. "I've never been special," he said bitterly. "I was turned by accident, a casualty of someone else's war. My immortality wasn't something I sought out it was forced on me. I'm not some chosen one, Helena. I'm just a vampire cursed to walk the earth forever."

But even as he said the words, a part of him knew that wasn't entirely true. He had always felt... different. From the moment he had been turned, there had been something inside him, something dark and powerful that he hadn't fully understood. Over the centuries, he had learned to control it, to live with it, but now he wondered if that power was something more than just his curse.

What if my immortality isn't just a curse? What if it's something else, something tied to the old ones?

The thought sent a chill down his spine. He didn't want to believe it, but the evidence was there, staring him in the face. His blood was the key. The book had said so. And if that was true, then there was something about him something about his very existence that was connected to these ancient creatures in ways he couldn't yet understand.

Isabelle reached out, her hand resting gently on his arm. "We'll figure it out, Silas," she said softly, her voice filled with quiet determination. "We always do."

Silas closed his eyes, leaning into her touch. Her presence, her love, was the only thing keeping him from spiralling into the abyss of his own fear. But even as she spoke those comforting words, he could feel the doubt gnawing at him. They had always managed to survive, always managed to find a way through the darkness. But this time... this time felt different.

What if there is no way through?

As the night wore on, they continued to pore over the book, searching for anything that could give them a clue, a hidden passage, a forgotten symbol, anything. But the more they read, the more it became clear that the book was not designed to help them. It was a warning. A prophecy of destruction.

"The old ones," Helena said slowly, reading another passage aloud, "do not dwell in this world as we know it. They are asleep, buried in the spaces between life and death, waiting for the blood that will call them forth. When they rise, the world will tremble, and the sky will darken with their shadow."

Silas's heart sank as he listened. The spaces between life and death. The words echoed in his mind, each one more ominous than the last. These creatures weren't hiding in some far-off place, waiting to be found. They were buried in the very fabric of reality, waiting to be awoken.

"How do we stop them from waking up?" Isabelle asked, her voice trembling slightly.

Helena looked up from the book, her expression grim. "I don't think we can."

Silas's chest tightened. He had feared as much. The old ones were beyond their reach, beyond their understanding. They existed outside the boundaries of life and death, and their power was far greater than anything Silas had ever encountered.

"They'll rise," Helena continued, her voice barely above a whisper. "When the balance of power is disrupted, when the blood of the cursed calls to them... they'll rise."

Silas stood abruptly; his hands clenched into fists. "So that's it?" he snapped, his voice filled with frustration. "We're supposed to just sit here and wait for them to tear the world apart? There has to be something we can do."

Helena shook her head, her expression filled with sorrow. "I don't know, Silas. This book doesn't offer a solution. It's a prophecy, not a guide. It tells us what's coming, but not how to stop it."

Silas turned away from the table, pacing the length of the room as his mind raced. The old ones were coming, and his blood was the key to their awakening. But he couldn't just stand by and let it happen. There had to be something they were missing, some way to stop the prophecy from being fulfilled.

But what?

Something about me, something about my blood, is connected to them. If they need my blood to rise... maybe there's a way to deny them.

The thought simmered in the back of his mind, but he pushed it aside. He wasn't ready to confront that possibility yet.

As he stood by the window, staring out into the dark streets of New York, Silas couldn't shake the feeling that time was running out. The old ones were stirring. And the longer they waited, the closer they came to waking.

The night passed in a blur of frantic research, but by dawn, they were no closer to finding the answers they needed. Silas sat by the window, watching the first light of morning creep over the horizon, his mind still spinning with the weight of the prophecy.

Why me? Why now?

He couldn't help but feel like a pawn in a game he didn't understand, caught in the middle of forces far greater than himself. The old ones were stirring, and it was his blood that would call them forth. The thought filled him with a deep, gnawing dread that he couldn't shake.

What if I'm the one who destroys everything?

And as the sun rose, casting a pale light over the city, Silas knew one thing for certain: they were running out of time.

Chapter Ten

The Weight of Uncertainty

The soft light of dawn crept through the heavy curtains of the mansion, casting long, golden beams across the room. The stillness that accompanied the day settled over the house like a blanket. It was the opposite of the restless, haunted nights that Silas and the others endured. Isabelle and Helena had finally fallen into a deep sleep, exhausted from hours of pouring over the ancient book, but Silas remained awake.

He hadn't slept not since they had returned from the library with the terrible knowledge that the old ones were stirring, waiting for his blood to call them forth. The house was eerily quiet during the day, the silence broken only by the occasional shifting of the wind outside. For most vampires, the daylight was a time of rest and recovery, the hours of safety when the sun would shield them from the dangers that lurked in the night. But for Silas, sleep was a luxury he couldn't afford.

He sat at the table, the ancient book spread open before him, its brittle pages glowing faintly in the daylight. The dim light that filtered through the windows made the text harder to read, the strange script shifting and twisting in ways that made his head ache. Silas rubbed his temples, frustration and exhaustion weighing heavily on him.

There has to be something I've missed, he thought, his eyes scanning the dark script for what felt like the hundredth time. Some clue. Some answer.

But the pages remained as cryptic as ever, offering no comfort, no solutions. Just the same grim prophecy of the old ones rising, of destruction and death following in their wake. His blood was the key to their awakening that much was clear. But the book offered no way to stop it, no way to fight back. It was as though the prophecy had already been written, and there was nothing left to do but wait for the end.

Surely, there must be something more. Silas leaned forward, his fingers tracing the sharp, angular symbols. He could feel the weight of the book, the power it held, but also the darkness that clung to it, as though it were alive with ancient knowledge too dangerous to fully reveal itself.

His thoughts churned with uncertainty, and with each passing hour, his frustration grew. He had always been a man of action, someone who fought his way through challenges. But this... this felt like a puzzle with pieces he didn't even know existed.

Why me? Why now?

The questions gnawed at him relentlessly. He had never considered himself special, never thought that his curse was anything more than bad luck. He had been turned into a vampire by chance, a victim of circumstance. But now, the more he thought about it, the more he began to wonder if there had been something more to his transformation. Something more to the curse that had been placed upon him.

Had my turning been part of a greater plan all along?

The idea sent a chill through him. He had always believed his transformation had been an accident an act of cruelty by the vampire who had attacked him. But what if there had been something else at work? What if his curse had been tied to the old ones from the beginning? The thought twisted in his mind, filling him with doubt and fear.

Silas leaned back in his chair, rubbing a hand over his face. His exhaustion was catching up to him, but his mind wouldn't let him rest. The images of the old ones the seven ancient beings described in the book played over and over again in his head. He could feel them, as though they were lurking just beneath the surface of the world, waiting to rise.

Why me? His thoughts spiralled, circling back to that question again and again. He had lived for centuries, wandering through the darkness, surviving as best he could. But now, everything felt different. He was no longer just a vampire cursed with immortality. He was something more something tied to forces beyond his understanding.

And that terrified him.

The hours dragged on, the soft ticking of a nearby clock marking the passage of time as Silas continued his fruitless search through the book. Isabelle and Helena remained asleep in the other room, their breathing steady and peaceful, while Silas's own heart pounded with anxiety. He had been up all day, pouring over the ancient text, searching for something anything that might give them an edge against the impending darkness.

But every page he turned was the same. No answers. No clues.

Just the same cryptic warning about the old ones and the blood of the cursed.

Silas closed the book, his hands trembling slightly. His eyes burned from exhaustion, but he couldn't stop. He wouldn't stop. Not when the lives of Isabelle and Helena were at stake. Not when the fate of the world hung in the balance.

Something about me... something about my past...

The thought hit him like a hammer. He had spent so long running from his past, from the memories of who he had been before he was turned, that he hadn't stopped to consider if there was something there something buried in his history that might hold the key to understanding why his blood was the one the old ones sought.

Surely, there must be something unusual about my family.

His memories of his mortal life were hazy, blurred by the centuries that had passed since he had walked the earth as a human. But he had never known much about his parents—only fragments, whispers of stories told to him as a child. His mother had died when he was young, and his father... his father had been a distant, shadowy figure, a man Silas had never truly known.

Who were they? What secrets did they hold?

Silas felt a strange sense of unease settle over him as he considered the possibility that his family his bloodline might be connected to the old ones. It seemed impossible, yet the more he thought about it, the more it made sense. If his blood was the key, then surely there had to be something about his heritage, something about his ancestors that had marked him for this fate.

He racked his brain, trying to recall any details about his family, but the memories were faint, almost non-existent. He had been so young when he was turned, so consumed by his new existence as a vampire, that he had never bothered to look back. But now, he realized how foolish that had been. His past might hold the answers he so desperately sought.

Silas's mind drifted back to the early days after he had been turned, to the years he had spent wandering the world, searching for purpose, for meaning. He had encountered many people along the way some who had helped him, others who had sought to use him. But there had been one man in particular, a vampire older than Silas had been at the time, who had taken an interest in him.

His name had been Marcel, a mysterious figure who had appeared out of nowhere, offering Silas guidance during his early years as a vampire. Marcel had been powerful, his presence commanding, with long, dark hair and piercing green eyes that seemed to see right through Silas. He had never revealed much about his past, but there had been something unsettling about him something that had always made Silas question his true motives.

Marcel had taken Silas under his wing, teaching him how to survive in the world of vampires, how to control his hunger, how to hide among humans. But there had always been an air of secrecy about Marcel, a sense that he knew more than he let on.

Something about him always felt... wrong.

Silas hadn't seen Marcel in centuries, but now, as he sat in the mansion, he couldn't shake the feeling that Marcel had known more about him than he had ever revealed. Had Marcel known about the connection between Silas's blood and the old ones? Had he been part of the reason Silas had been marked for this fate?

The thought made Silas's stomach churn with unease. He had trusted Marcel once, but now, looking back, he realized that Marcel had always kept him at arm's length, never revealing his true intentions. Perhaps Marcel had been part of a larger plan, a plan to awaken the old ones.

So many lies. So many secrets.

Silas stood abruptly, pacing the length of the room as his thoughts raced. If Marcel had known about the connection between Silas's blood and the old ones, then there had to be others, other vampires, other beings who were involved. Perhaps Ambrose wasn't the only one who had been watching him, waiting for the right moment to strike.

The weight of it all pressed down on Silas like a crushing force. His mind was a whirlwind of conflicting thoughts, doubts, and fears. He had always believed he was alone in his curse, that he had been turned by accident. But now, he wasn't so sure. There were too many unanswered questions, too many things that didn't add up.

Who am I, really?

As the hours dragged on, Silas continued to search the book, but his frustration only grew. Every passage he read seemed to lead him further into the darkness, offering no solutions, no hope. He felt as though he were drowning, trapped in a sea of ancient knowledge that refused to reveal its secrets.

The clock ticked softly in the background, marking the passing of time, but Silas hardly noticed. His mind was consumed by the questions that had plagued him for centuries. Who were his parents? What was his true lineage? And how did it connect to the old ones?

By the time the sun began to set, casting long shadows across the room, Silas was no closer to finding the answers he needed. Isabelle and Helena began to stir, their sleep undisturbed by the weight of the day's revelations. But Silas felt no peace. His mind was still racing, still searching for the key that would unlock the mysteries of his past.

And as the darkness of night began to creep back into the world, Silas knew one thing for certain: the answers he sought were not in the book. They were buried in his past; hidden in the shadows of the life he had left behind.

It's time to face the truth. No more running.

Chapter Eleven

Uncovering the Past

The soft, ambient light of the mansion cast shadows across the room as Silas sat in silence, the weight of his newfound knowledge pressing down on him. The night stretched on, but sleep was the furthest thing from his mind. His thoughts raced, each one tugging him back to his past, searching for clues, for anything he might have missed about his family. The discovery of his bloodline's connection to the old ones gnawed at him relentlessly. There had to be something he'd overlooked, something hidden in the memories of his mortal life.

He tried to recall the vague memories he had of his mother, a woman with soft, kind eyes and a gentle voice that had soothed him as a child. She had died when he was young, her passing shrouded in mystery. And then there was his father, a distant, cold man whose face he could barely remember, like a shadow lurking in the corners of his mind. They had raised him in silence, their affection scarce, their past even scarcer. He had always felt like an outsider, different from them in ways he hadn't understood. Even as a child, there had been a strange sense of detachment, as though he was merely a guest in their lives.

But was there something else, something he had missed in his search for belonging?

Why didn't they tell me more? The thought surfaced, sharp and bitter. He had accepted their silence, their refusal to speak of their own past, as simply the way things were. He had never questioned it...not until now. His curse, his immortality... if it was tied to something older, something far beyond himself, then maybe his family had known. Maybe they had hidden the truth from him.

So many years wasted, so many centuries lost in the dark... Was I destined for this all along?

A knock on the door pulled him from his thoughts. Helena stepped into the room, her eyes wide and filled with a strange urgency. She looked different....paler than usual, as though she had just woken from a vivid dream or vision.

"Silas," she began, her voice trembling slightly. "I need to speak with you."

Silas looked up, his gaze sharp. Helena's face was drawn, her eyes shadowed with a mix of fear and anticipation. He could see that something had shaken her, something beyond the usual stress of their current situation.

"Helena," he said, his tone cautious. "What is it?"

She stepped closer, her expression intense as she spoke. "I had a vision," she said softly, her voice barely above a whisper. "It came to me just now. I saw... I saw you, Silas. And I saw your bloodline. But it wasn't what you think."

Silas frowned, his pulse quickening. "What do you mean?"

Helena took a steadying breath. "Your parents, the ones who raised you... they're not your true family. They're not your biological parents. I saw it in the vision. You're from a different bloodline, a line tied to royalty a line connected to something much older, much darker than any of us realized."

Silas's mind reeled, her words striking him like a blow. For as long as he could remember, he had thought of his parents as his true family, albeit a distant, cold one. The idea that they weren't his real parents, that his true lineage was tied to something far more ancient left him speechless.

"That's impossible," he said, though the words felt hollow even as he spoke them. Deep down, he had always sensed there was something different about him. He had always felt like an outsider, like a piece that didn't quite fit.

Helena's gaze softened, her eyes filled with sympathy. "I know it's hard to believe, Silas. But the vision was clear. Your true parents... they come from a royal bloodline, one that was thought to be lost centuries ago. And it's that bloodline that connects you to the old ones. It's not your curse that binds you to them it's your heritage."

Silas felt his chest tighten, his mind racing as he tried to process what she was saying. He had spent centuries haunted by the idea that his curse was a punishment, a twist of fate that had marked him as different. But now, Helena was telling him that it wasn't the curse itself it was something far deeper. It was in his blood.

He looked away, his mind filled with memories of his childhood, of the cold, distant figures who had raised him. Had they known? Had they hidden the truth from him all along?

"Why didn't they tell me?" he murmured, his voice thick with emotion. "If they knew... why didn't they say anything?"

Helena placed a hand on his shoulder, her touch gentle but grounding. "Maybe they were trying to protect you," she said softly. "Or maybe they didn't know the full extent of what you were. Royal bloodlines are often shrouded in secrecy. They're guarded, hidden away. And if your true family was tied to the old ones... it's possible that they were trying to shield you from that knowledge."

Silas closed his eyes, his mind racing as he tried to make sense of everything. He had always felt like there was something different about him, something that set him apart from others, even before he had been turned. But he had never imagined that it was because of his bloodline, because of a lineage that connected him to creatures as ancient as the old ones.

His thoughts drifted to the faces of the people who had shaped his early years, shadowy figures from his past who had drifted in and out of his life like phantoms. There had been a man named Mathias, a family friend who had visited them often. Mathias had been a dark, imposing figure, with piercing eyes that seemed to see right through him. Silas had always felt a strange sense of fear around Mathias, as though the man knew something he didn't.

And then there was Eveline, a woman who had been his mother's closest friend. Eveline had been a quiet, mysterious figure, with a beauty that was both mesmerizing and unsettling. She had never spoken much to Silas, but he remembered the way she would watch him, her gaze filled with an intensity that had always made him uncomfortable.

Was it all connected? Silas wondered, his mind reeling with the implications. Had they known about his true heritage? Had they been involved in whatever secrets his family had hidden from him?

"Helena," he said, his voice strained. "What else did you see in the vision? Was there anything about where I come from? Anything about my true parents?"

Helena hesitated, her gaze distant as she recalled the details of the vision. "There was a name," she said finally, her voice soft. "I heard it whispered, like an echo. The House of Shere. I don't know what it means, but it felt... ancient. Powerful."

Silas felt a chill run down his spine at the name. The House of Shere. It sounded like something out of a forgotten legend, a name that carried a weight of history and mystery. He had never heard of it before, but the sound of it resonated with him, as though it were a part of him he had long forgotten.

He glanced at Helena, his expression a mix of disbelief and wonder. "So, you're telling me that I'm... royalty? That my bloodline is connected to some ancient house tied to the old ones?"

Helena nodded, her eyes filled with sympathy. "Yes, Silas. That's exactly what I'm saying."

Silas sat down, his mind spinning. The revelation left him feeling both awe and fear. He had spent so long believing that his curse was a fluke, a twist of fate that had marked him for eternity. But now, he realized that it was something far more intentional, something that had been woven into his very blood.

"What do we do now?" Isabelle asked, her voice barely above a whisper.

Silas looked up at her, his gaze filled with determination. "We find out more. About The House of Shere, about my true heritage, and about how it connects to the old ones."

Helena nodded, her expression resolute. "I'll look through every ancient text we have, search for any mention of the Shere name. If there's any record of this bloodline, I'll find it."

Isabelle placed a hand on Silas's shoulder, her touch grounding him. "We're with you," she said softly. "No matter where this takes us, we're with you."

Silas took a steadying breath, feeling the weight of their support. He had spent centuries alone, isolated by his curse. But now, he had something he had never truly allowed himself before true companions. Allies who were willing to face the darkness with him.

And as he looked around the room, at the faces of the people who had become his family, he felt a spark of hope. For the first time in centuries, he wasn't alone in his fight. They were in this together, and he would do everything in his power to uncover the truth of his past, no matter where it led.

Because he knew now that the answers they sought weren't just about his curse. They were about something much bigger, a legacy that was tied to the fate of the world itself.

Chapter Twelve

Unveiling the Past

The candlelight flickered softly in the dim study, casting shadows that danced across the walls and draping the room in a warm, quiet glow. Silas sat in silence, his gaze distant, as he wrestled with the weight of everything he'd just learned. His heritage, once thought to be so simple, so ordinary, was bound to a legacy older than he'd ever imagined. The House of Shere an ancient bloodline tied to the dark forces of the old ones, a lineage steeped in power and mystery.

Across the room, Helena was busy at work, her sharp eyes scanning the spines of the countless books lining the shelves of his extensive library. She moved with purpose, her movements quick and sure, as though she was chasing a thought that wouldn't rest until she unearthed every truth. In the corner, Isabelle sat quietly, her face pale with the weight of the revelations they had uncovered. Helena had shared something with her, something about her own heritage, a connection to Silas's past that neither of them had anticipated.

Helena glanced back at Isabelle, her expression thoughtful. "It's strange," she said quietly. "Your family... there's a connection between your heritage and Silas's bloodline, though I can't fully explain it yet."

Silas's attention sharpened, his gaze flicking between Helena and Isabelle. "What are you talking about?" he asked, his voice low.

Helena sighed, running a hand through her hair as she leaned against one of the shelves. "I didn't mention it earlier," she began, her voice hesitant, "but there are legends... myths, really, that speak of two souls bound together across lifetimes. In some of the ancient texts I've read, it's said that certain bloodlines carry the essence of these souls, meant to find each other in every life, regardless of time or circumstance."

Isabelle's eyes widened, a spark of recognition flashing in her gaze. "You mean... you think Silas and I—"

Helena nodded slowly. "It's possible. There's something in your family history that echoes his, as though the two of you are connected across centuries. I haven't found anything definitive yet, but I've always suspected that your bloodlines... they're intertwined somehow, part of a larger design. It's likely that you were meant to find each other."

Silas's heart thudded heavily in his chest at her words. He had always felt an undeniable pull toward Isabelle, a connection that defied logic or reason. But to hear Helena say it aloud, to suggest that their bond was something more than chance, left him feeling both exhilarated and fearful. Could it be true? Had they truly known each other in past lives, destined to find each other over and over again?

But as quickly as the thought took hold, Silas pushed it aside. He couldn't allow himself to get lost in dreams of past lives and fated love. Not when the threat of the old ones loomed over them, dark and unstoppable. He forced himself to stay focused, to push aside the emotions that swirled inside him.

"We'll keep it to ourselves," Silas said firmly, his gaze locking onto Helena's. "No need to bring Isabelle into this any more than she already is. There's enough to worry about without dragging her into the depths of whatever this... connection might mean."

Isabelle's mouth opened as though she wanted to protest, but she remained silent, her eyes filled with a quiet determination that mirrored his own. He knew she wouldn't push him, but the look in her eyes told him that she wouldn't let it go, either.

Helena nodded, though Silas could see the unease flickering across her face. "Very well," she said, her tone resigned. "But this isn't something we can ignore forever, Silas. The truth will find a way to reveal itself, whether we're ready for it or not."

Hours passed in silence, each of them lost in thought as they tried to process the revelations that had been uncovered. The night deepened, its stillness broken only by the soft sounds of pages turning as Helena continued her search through the library's vast collection. She had an intensity about her, a focus that was almost unnerving, as though she were following a trail that only she could see.

And then, finally, she let out a soft gasp, her fingers trailing over the spine of a dusty, ancient tome she had found tucked away on one of the higher shelves. She carefully pulled the book from its place, cradling it in her hands as though it were a fragile artifact.

Silas's gaze shifted to the book, a sense of recognition sparking in his mind as he took in the worn cover, the faded lettering. It was one of the oldest books in his collection, one he had almost forgotten existed. He had collected it centuries ago, during his travels in Eastern Europe, but he had never taken the time to truly study it.

Helena looked up at him, her eyes wide. "This might be it," she whispered. "The book we need."

Silas moved closer, his heart pounding as he examined the cover. The title was inscribed in an old dialect, but he recognized it immediately. "Chronicles of the Shere Bloodline"—a record of his lineage, hidden in plain sight within his own library.

Helena opened the book, her fingers trailing over the brittle pages as she carefully flipped through the text. The inscriptions were written in a mixture of languages, some he recognized, others he had never seen before. But the essence of it was clear the book was a history of the House of Shere, his true heritage, detailing the origins of his bloodline and its connection to the old ones.

She stopped at a page, her finger resting on an inscription written in dark, flowing script. The words were sharp, almost violent in appearance, and Silas felt a chill run down his spine as he read them.

"In darkness they were bound, in blood they shall rise. The House of Shere, marked by fate, shall awaken the old ones and stand as the gate."

The words echoed in his mind, a foreboding chant that filled him with a sense of dread. He could feel the power of the words, the weight of the prophecy that lay upon his bloodline. It was as though his very existence had been predetermined, his fate sealed long before he had even been born.

The House of Shere, marked by fate, shall awaken the old ones and stand as the gate.

Silas's jaw tightened, his mind racing with the implications. He had always felt different, set apart from others by his curse. But now he realized that it was more than just the curse that marked him it was his blood, his heritage. He was bound to the old ones, connected to them by a destiny he couldn't escape.

Helena's eyes were filled with awe as she continued to read, her voice soft but steady. "It says here that the House of Shere was founded centuries ago, by a royal family that held power over life and death itself. They were feared, revered as both rulers and gods. The Morrigans had a power unlike any other a power tied to the old ones, creatures so ancient that they existed before time itself."

Silas felt a wave of anger surge through him, his fists clenching as he struggled to control his emotions. Why was this kept from me? Why didn't anyone tell me the truth about who I am? The anger was tempered by a deep sadness, a longing for the life he had once known, the simplicity of his mortal days. But that life was gone, replaced by a destiny he could neither deny nor escape.

"What else does it say?" Isabelle asked, her voice barely more than a whisper.

Helena glanced at her, then looked back at the book, her expression somber. "The House of Shere was destroyed," she continued. "Centuries ago, its members scattered, hunted down by those who feared their power. But the bloodline survived, passed down through generations, hidden in secret, waiting for the time when it would be needed again."

Silas's heart sank at her words. His bloodline had been hunted, erased from history, hidden away like a dark secret. And now, he was the last of that line, the final heir to a power he neither wanted nor understood.

Helena closed the book gently, her gaze meeting his. "You're not just a vampire, Silas. You're the heir to a legacy older than the world itself. The House of Shere was meant to stand between the old ones and the mortal world. And now... it falls to you."

Silas let out a slow breath, his mind churning with emotions he couldn't name. He felt a mixture of pride and horror, a sense of belonging and isolation. He had always known he was different, that there was something in him that set him apart from others. But he had never imagined it would be this.

He looked at Isabelle, her face pale with shock, her sapphire eyes filled with worry. She had been his anchor, the one person who had given him a reason to keep going. But now, he wondered if his connection to her was part of this twisted fate if she, too, was bound to the old ones through her bloodline.

Helena closed the book and looked at them both, her expression serious. "We have a choice to make," she said quietly. "We can fight this, try to find a way to stop the old ones from rising. Or... we can accept what's coming and prepare ourselves to face it."

Silas felt a surge of resolve, his determination hardening like steel. He would not be a pawn in some ancient game, a tool for forces he didn't understand. He would fight. He would protect Isabelle, protect those he loved, even if it meant defying his own fate.

"We keep this to ourselves," he said firmly, his gaze locking onto Helena's. "We don't tell anyone else about the Shere bloodline, or about our connection to the old ones. Not yet. We need to understand more before we act."

Helena nodded, though he could see the unease flickering in her eyes. "Agreed," she replied. "But remember, Silas... this isn't something we can run from forever. The old ones are coming. And when they do, we'll have to be ready."

Silas looked down at the closed book, his hand resting on its cover as though it held the answers he so desperately sought. The legacy of the Shere bloodline lay within him, an ancient power he could not deny. And now, it was up to him to decide how to wield it.

For the first time in his life, Silas felt the weight of his heritage, the strength of the blood that coursed through his veins. He was no longer just a vampire cursed with immortality. He was the last of the Sheres, a guardian standing between the old ones and the world they sought to consume.

And as he looked at Isabelle, at the woman he loved, he knew that he would do whatever it took to protect her, even if it meant facing the ancient forces that waited in the shadows.

Chapter Thirteen

Echoes of the Past

The night was quiet, the air in the mansion thick with the weight of everything Silas had uncovered. His mind was restless, filled with images and memories that danced just beyond his reach, fragments of a life he had only begun to understand. He stood by the large window, staring out into the darkness, his reflection barely visible against the glass. The House of Morrigan, his true bloodline, was a legacy he had never asked for, a history he had never known. And now, that heritage loomed over him, stretching back through the centuries, binding him to the ancient forces that waited to rise.

In the silence, he could feel the tug of memories he had long since buried, remnants of his early childhood that he had tried to forget. Images flickered through his mind like distant echoes, his mother's soft face, the way her dark hair had fallen around her shoulders like a veil; his father's stern gaze, his quiet but commanding presence. They had always felt like strangers to him, shadows in a life he had barely lived before he was turned.

But now, he wondered if they had known. If they had hidden the truth from him, concealing the power that lay within his blood. His heart clenched as he remembered the cold distance between them, the way they had always kept him at arm's length, never quite letting him in. Was it because of the Shere bloodline? Had they feared what he was, even then?

What did they know? What were they hiding from me?

He closed his eyes, allowing the memories to wash over him, fragments of his childhood drifting to the surface. He remembered a summer evening, the warm glow of the setting sun casting long shadows over the garden. He had been no more than five or six, playing among the flowers as his mother watched from a distance. She had been beautiful, with dark eyes that held a depth he hadn't understood at the time, a sadness that had always lingered behind her gentle smile.

And then there was Mathias, his father's closest friend, a tall, imposing man with a deep voice and eyes that gleamed with a strange intensity. Mathias had always made him uneasy, though he hadn't known why. As a child, he had only sensed the tension in the man's gaze, the way he watched Silas with a mix of curiosity and wariness, as though he were waiting for something to reveal itself.

Mathias knew, Silas thought bitterly. He could feel it now, the certainty settling over him like a shadow. Mathias had known about his heritage, about the power that lay dormant within him. And instead of helping him understand, instead of guiding him, the man had watched him from a distance, treating him like an experiment, a curiosity.

His chest tightened with anger and betrayal. His entire life had been shaped by secrets, by people who had hidden the truth from him, and now those secrets were coming back to haunt him. All those years spent in the dark, and for what?

The memories shifted, drifting further back to fragments he could barely piece together. He remembered Eveline, his mother's closest friend, a woman with striking beauty and a quiet, haunting presence. She had always treated him kindly, but there had been something unsettling in her gaze, as though she, too, saw something in him that he couldn't yet understand. She had spoken to him in riddles, her words soft and cryptic, leaving him confused and frustrated.

As a child, he had dismissed it, thinking it was just the way adults were distant and mysterious, keeping their own secrets. But now, looking back, he could see the truth. Eveline had known, just like Mathias. They had all known.

So many years wasted, he thought bitterly. So many lives built on lies.

He clenched his fists, his body tense with anger and frustration. The weight of his heritage, the truth of his bloodline, was a burden he could barely comprehend, let alone accept. He had spent centuries wandering, believing himself to be cursed, never knowing that his very existence was bound to something far darker, far older.

And then a new thought surfaced, one that sent a chill through him, filling him with doubt and unease.

Are these my memories? Or are they someone else's?

The question gnawed at him, filling him with a sense of dread. He had always known that vampires could share memories, could implant images and thoughts into each other's minds. But he had never experienced it himself, never felt the strange, unsettling sensation of another's mind merging with his own.

Could someone be reaching into my thoughts? Could they be planting these memories, making me see things that aren't really mine?

The thought sent a shiver down his spine, and he opened his eyes, his gaze fixed on the darkness outside. The memories felt real, tangible, but there was a part of him that couldn't shake the feeling that they were being manipulated, twisted by someone else's influence.

"Silas?"

The soft voice broke through his thoughts, pulling him back to the present. Isabelle stood beside him, her hand resting gently on his arm. He hadn't heard her enter, so lost had he been in the shadows of his own mind.

She reached up, pressing a soft kiss to his temple, her warmth grounding him, pulling him out of the spiral of memories and doubts that had consumed him. He closed his eyes, savoring the comfort of her touch, the familiarity of her presence. She was his anchor, the one person who had seen him for who he truly was, without the weight of his past or the shadows of his bloodline.

"Are you alright?" she asked softly, her gaze filled with concern.

Silas let out a slow breath, his shoulders relaxing under her touch. "I don't know," he admitted, his voice barely above a whisper. "I keep remembering things, fragments of my childhood. But I don't know if they're real. I don't know if they're mine."

Isabelle's brow furrowed, and she took his hand, her fingers lacing through his. "What do you mean?"

Silas hesitated, his mind racing as he tried to find the words. "Vampires... we can share memories, implant images into each other's minds. I keep seeing things, memories of my parents, of people I barely remember. But I don't know if they're mine, or if someone else is... pushing them into my mind."

The words hung between them, heavy and filled with uncertainty. Isabelle's gaze softened, her hand tightening around his as she looked up at him. "If these memories are yours, then you'll know, deep down. No one else can tell you what's real, Silas. Only you can decide that."

Her words, simple as they were, brought him a measure of comfort, though the doubts still lingered. He wanted to believe that these memories were his, that they were fragments of his true past, his true heritage. But the fear of manipulation, of someone reaching into his mind, refused to leave him.

What if this is all a lie?

He pushed the thought aside, unwilling to let it consume him. There was too much at stake, too many questions left unanswered. If these memories were real, then they held the key to understanding his connection to the old ones, to the House of Shere . He had to trust himself, to trust his own mind, even if it meant walking a path shrouded in uncertainty.

Isabelle's hand remained in his, her warmth a steadying presence as they stood together in the quiet of the room. He looked down at her, his heart aching with gratitude for her support, her unwavering faith in him.

"Thank you," he murmured, his voice rough with emotion. "For being here. For... everything."

Isabelle smiled, her gaze filled with love and understanding. "You don't have to thank me, Silas. I'm with you, no matter where this journey takes us. Whatever you face, you won't face it alone."

He nodded, his heart swelling with a mixture of gratitude and sorrow. He had spent so many years alone, burdened by a curse he hadn't understood, haunted by memories he had tried to forget. But now, for the first time, he felt as though he wasn't alone. He had Isabelle, Helena, and the truth of his bloodline guiding him, even as the shadows grew darker.

And as he looked back at the mansion, at the home he had built in isolation, he felt a flicker of hope, hope that he could finally uncover the truth, that he could finally face the darkness that had haunted him for so long.

But even as he clung to that hope, the doubt lingered, whispering in the back of his mind.

Were these memories real, or were they a trap?

Only time would tell. And as the night stretched on, Silas knew that the answers he sought lay within him, waiting to be uncovered, waiting to reveal the true legacy of the House of Shere.

Chapter Fourteen

The Gathering Shadows

The mansion lay in silence, the weight of ancient secrets pressing down on its stone walls. The night was thick and still, cloaked in the kind of darkness that seemed to swallow everything in its path. Silas stood in the grand foyer, his mind a storm of thoughts and emotions he couldn't shake. He needed air, a moment alone to make sense of everything he had learned. Gently, he slipped away from Isabelle and Helena, who sat in quiet conversation in the drawing room, their voices hushed as if in respect for the heaviness that surrounded them all.

Stepping outside, he let the cold night air wash over him, grounding him in the present, pulling him from the swirling tide of memories and revelations that threatened to drown him. He began to walk, his footsteps echoing softly against the cobbled streets. New York City, for all its lights and life, felt eerily empty tonight, the usual noise and clamor muted as though the world itself held its breath.

Silas's thoughts turned inward, and he found himself reflecting on everything that had happened over the past few nights. The discovery of his true heritage, the connection to the old ones, Isabelle's own mysterious ties to his bloodline, each revelation had shaken the foundations of his existence. He had spent centuries believing he was cursed, an outsider destined to walk the world alone, haunted by shadows of his past. But now, he was beginning to understand that he had been a part of something far larger all along, bound to ancient forces that had shaped his fate long before he'd taken his first breath.

And yet, as much as he tried to piece together the fragments of his history, the answers seemed to slip through his fingers, like sand in an hourglass. Each revelation only brought more questions, and with each step he took, he felt as though he were walking deeper into the darkness, a labyrinth with no end in sight.

Is this who I am meant to be? he wondered, his gaze fixed on the ground. Or am I just a pawn in a game I can't hope to understand?

The weight of his heritage, the power of the House of Shere, pressed heavily upon him. He had never asked for this, never wanted to be tied to creatures as ancient and powerful as the old ones. But it was in his blood, woven into the very essence of who he was. And now, he had no choice but to confront it.

He stopped, his gaze lifting to the sky, where the stars hung like distant memories. In the stillness, he felt a strange sense of clarity, a calm that he hadn't experienced in years. His path was set, whether he liked it or not. The old ones were stirring, and he was the key to their awakening. But he wouldn't face it alone. Isabelle, Helena, and perhaps even others who shared his cause, they would stand by his side. He would not let fear dictate his fate.

Just as he was beginning to feel the weight lift, a figure emerged from the shadows ahead, stepping into the faint glow of a nearby streetlamp. Silas's senses sharpened, his body tensing as he prepared for anything. But as the figure drew closer, a sense of familiarity washed over him, easing his tension.

"Silas," the man greeted, his voice a soft, rich baritone that held a hint of warmth. His face was partially hidden beneath the brim of a dark hat, his coat long and flowing, giving him an almost ghostly appearance. But his eyes, sharp, piercing gray were unmistakable.

"Ronan?" Silas's voice was barely more than a whisper, a mix of surprise and relief coloring his tone.

Ronan inclined his head, a faint smile playing on his lips. "It's been a long time, old friend."

Silas felt a surge of emotion he hadn't expected. Ronan had been a friend and ally during some of the darkest years of his life, a fellow vampire who had shared his journey through the shadows. They had parted ways centuries ago, each of them drawn by their own paths, their own battles. But seeing him now, here in New York, felt like a reminder of the past he had tried so hard to bury.

"You've changed," Silas murmured, studying the man before him. Ronan's face was still youthful, but there was a depth in his eyes, a weight that hadn't been there before. His once carefree nature had been replaced by something darker, something older, as though he had seen more than he was willing to speak of.

"We all have," Ronan replied softly, his gaze steady. "These are dark times, Silas. The old ones... their stirrings reach far beyond this city."

Silas nodded, his own fears reflected in his friend's words. "You've felt it too, then? The awakening?"

Ronan's expression grew serious, and he stepped closer, his voice barely above a whisper. "It's more than just an awakening, Silas. They're preparing to rise, and their power stretches far beyond anything you or I have encountered. But you're not alone in this fight.

There are others, those who would stand with you, those who have been waiting for this moment."

Silas's heart quickened at his words. "Others? Who?"

Ronan's gaze softened, and for a moment, Silas saw a flicker of the man he had once known, the friend who had stood beside him in battles long past, who had shared his pain and his triumphs. "There are those who remember the old ways," he said, his voice low and steady. "Those who have lived long enough to see the world change, who understand the threat the old ones pose. Some of them have sworn to protect the world from forces like these, even if it means risking their own lives."

Silas's mind raced, his thoughts filled with images of ancient vampires, warriors who had spent centuries honing their skills, preparing for a battle that had been prophesied long ago. The idea of others vampires and creatures who shared his purpose filled him with a renewed sense of hope.

"Why haven't I heard of this?" Silas asked, his voice a mixture of curiosity and disbelief. "If there are others, why haven't they come forward?"

Ronan's expression grew somber. "Because they needed to be certain, Silas. The old ones are not to be taken lightly, and they will not risk exposing themselves unless they know the threat is real. But now... now there is no doubt. The House of Shere is the key, and you, Silas, are the last of that bloodline."

Silas felt a chill run through him, the weight of his heritage settling over him once again. He had always felt alone, a solitary figure wandering through the darkness. But now, he realized that there were others who shared his burden, who understood the path he was destined to walk.

Ronan placed a hand on his shoulder, his grip firm and steady. "You are not alone in this, old friend. When the time comes, we will stand with you. There is a gathering happening, a calling of the ancient ones who still remember the darkness. When the moment is right, we will find you. And together, we will face whatever comes."

Silas's heart swelled with gratitude, a feeling he hadn't allowed himself to experience in a long time. He looked at Ronan, the friend who had reappeared from the shadows just when he needed him most, and he felt a surge of strength, a reminder that he was not as isolated as he had believed.

"Thank you, Ronan," Silas said quietly, his voice filled with emotion. "I... I didn't realize how much I needed to hear that."

Ronan's faint smile returned, his eyes filled with warmth and understanding. "We all need reminders, Silas. No one can carry this burden alone. Not even you."

They stood in silence, the quiet of the night wrapping around them like a shroud. Silas felt a sense of peace settle over him, a calm that he hadn't known in years. For the first time, he felt as though he wasn't just a pawn in a game of shadows and ancient power. He was part of something larger, something that had been waiting for him all along.

Ronan took a step back, his form already beginning to blend into the darkness. "Until we meet again, old friend," he said softly, his voice like a whisper carried on the wind. "When the time is right."

And with that, he was gone, disappearing into the shadows as though he had never been there. Silas watched the empty space where his friend had stood, his heart pounding with a mixture of hope and anticipation.

He was not alone. There were others, warriors and allies, who understood the fight that lay ahead. And when the time came, they would stand with him, ready to face the ancient forces that threatened to rise.

As he turned to make his way back to the mansion, a renewed sense of purpose filled him. He was the last of the House of Shere, a guardian of a legacy that had been hidden for centuries. But he was no longer just a lone figure walking through the darkness. He was part of something greater, a force that would stand against the old ones when the time came.

And as he walked, his mind clearer than it had been in days, he whispered a silent promise to himself, to Isabelle, to Helena, and to all those who would stand with him.

I will face whatever comes. And I will not falter.

Chapter Fifteen

Shadows and Echoes

Silas walked slowly back toward the mansion, his thoughts swirling as he replayed the night's events over and over in his mind. The encounter with Ronan had stirred up emotions he hadn't allowed himself to feel in centuries, a mixture of relief, hope, and a sense of companionship he had thought lost to him. Ronan's words echoed in his mind, the promise of others who would stand with him when the time came, a reminder that he wasn't as alone in this fight as he had believed.

But beneath that hope lay a simmering uncertainty. Ronan was no ordinary vampire. He had been a part of Silas's life during some of the most difficult years, an ally and confidant, but also a mystery wrapped in layers of silence and shadows. Silas had trusted him once, long ago, and yet he couldn't help but wonder if there was more to his reappearance than a simple reunion of old friends.

As he neared the mansion, a whisper floated through his mind, soft and chilling as though carried on the wind.

"Be careful of your thoughts, my friend. There are enemies lurking in the shadows, waiting for the right moment to strike. They would see you destroyed, and with you, all that remains of the Shere bloodline."

Silas froze, his heart pounding as he recognized Ronan's voice, a phantom in his mind. He could feel the weight of the warning, the urgency in his friend's words. Ronan was right the old ones weren't the only threat. There were others, enemies who had been watching from the darkness, waiting for an opportunity to strike. Silas's heritage, his connection to the Shere bloodline, had made him a target long before he had even understood what that legacy meant.

He let out a slow breath, his gaze shifting to the shadows that stretched across the empty street. The night felt heavier now, the familiar darkness suddenly filled with unseen eyes and hidden threats. He couldn't shake the feeling that he was being watched, that every step he took was marked by forces he couldn't see.

Enemies lurking in the shadows. Ronan's words played over in his mind, a warning that lingered like smoke in the air. It had been centuries since Silas had last seen his old friend, and their reunion had been brief, but it had stirred memories he had tried to leave behind. Memories of a time when he had been new to this life, lost and searching for purpose, when Ronan had stepped in, guiding him through the darkness.

Ronan had been a friend, yes, but more than that, he had been a mentor. A vampire older and more experienced, who had taken Silas under his wing during those early years of confusion and isolation. But Ronan himself was a complex figure, a man whose past was shrouded in secrecy. Silas had known only fragments of his story, pieces of a life that seemed to stretch back farther than even he could comprehend.

Before he had been turned, Ronan had been a knight, a protector sworn to uphold a code of honor. He had been born in the early days of medieval Europe, a time of wars and bloodshed, of feudal lords and castles. Silas remembered the stories Ronan had shared, tales of battles fought and kingdoms defended, of oaths made and broken. There had been a quiet nobility about him, a sense of duty that had carried over even after he was turned. He had been turned during a time of great conflict, in the aftermath of a battle that had left him wounded and near death. A vampire, one he had never named, had come to him in his final moments, offering him a choice, a second life, a life in darkness.

Ronan had accepted, not out of fear or desperation, but out of a sense of duty. He had believed that he could use his new abilities to protect those who could not protect themselves, to continue his life's purpose in a new, darker form. But over the centuries, that sense of duty had shifted, changed by the weight of immortality, by the endless cycle of war and bloodshed that followed him wherever he went.

And now, after all this time, he had returned, a ghost from Silas's past, offering his help in the fight against the old ones.

Silas, Ronan's voice whispered again, breaking through his thoughts, there are forces at play that you cannot yet see. Trust no one, not fully. The old ones are not our only enemies.

Silas clenched his jaw, a wave of frustration washing over him. He had spent so much of his life surrounded by secrets and shadows, by half-truths and hidden motives. Even now, with the weight of his heritage pressing down on him, he felt as though he were still being kept in the dark, still a pawn in a game he didn't understand.

Why did you come back, Ronan? he thought, a sense of bitterness creeping into his mind. What are you hiding?

Despite his frustration, Silas couldn't deny the comfort he felt in knowing that Ronan was there, that he was watching, even if from a distance. They had been through so much together, fought battles side by side, trusted each other in ways that few others could understand. But Ronan had always been a mystery, a man of shadows who seemed to appear and disappear as though guided by some unseen hand.

As he reached the mansion, Silas took a deep breath, trying to calm the storm inside him. He needed to keep his mind clear, to stay focused on the fight ahead. Ronan's warning echoed in his thoughts, a reminder of the dangers that lurked in the dark corners of his world. He couldn't afford to let his guard down, not now, not with the old ones stirring, not with enemies hidden in the shadows.

Silas pushed open the door to the mansion, stepping into the quiet of the foyer. The familiar stillness of the house wrapped around him, grounding him, pulling him from the depths of his thoughts. But even as he closed the door behind him, he could still feel the weight of Ronan's words, a silent reminder of the dangers that lay ahead.

And as he stood in the darkness, his mind still swirling with memories and doubts, he whispered a silent promise to himself, a vow that echoed through the empty halls of the mansion.

If enemies wait for me in the shadows, then let them come. I will be ready.

Chapter Sixteen

A Love That Endures

Silas closed the door softly behind him, the weight of the night settling over him like a cloak. He had left the darkened streets behind, yet shadows clung to him, the reminders of all that he had learned and all that he was yet to face. His thoughts were still thick with Ronan's warnings, the lurking dangers that waited in the corners of his world. But now, as he stepped into the warm glow of the drawing room, all of that faded into the background.

There, seated by the window, was Isabelle. The soft lamplight illuminated her face, casting a gentle glow over her delicate features. Her hair fell in loose waves over her shoulders, and her eyes, a striking shade of sapphire, were focused on a book in her hands. She looked up as he entered, her gaze meeting his, and in that moment, everything else fell away. There was a calm in her presence, a strength that reached out to him and reminded him why he had fought so hard, why he would continue to fight even against the darkness that loomed on the horizon.

Without a word, Silas moved toward her, each step deliberate, as though he were drawn to her by something he couldn't resist. She closed the book, setting it aside as he approached, and her eyes softened, her lips curving into a gentle smile that made his heart ache with a fierce, undeniable longing. He extended a hand, his fingers brushing against hers, warm and inviting. She didn't hesitate, placing her hand in his as he gently guided her up from the chair, her body moving fluidly into his embrace.

For a moment, they stood in silence, caught in the closeness that bound them together in ways words could never express. Silas looked down at her, his hand resting lightly on her waist as he gazed into her eyes, each heartbeat echoing the depth of his emotions. He could feel the intensity of his love for her, a passion that had survived centuries of darkness, of loneliness and pain. Isabelle was the light in his life, the one constant that had kept him grounded, even when he had been lost in the shadows.

He moved closer, his face inches from hers, his gaze falling to her lips. He felt a surge of emotion, a longing that filled him with both anticipation and a fierce need to protect her from everything that threatened their love. He hesitated, savoring the moment, the anticipation that hung between them like a charged current. And then, slowly, he closed the distance, his lips brushing against hers in a kiss that was tender and filled with all the unspoken words he had held inside.

The kiss deepened, their passion igniting as if a fire had been sparked between them. Silas's hand moved to the back of her neck, holding her gently as he pulled her closer, his heart pounding with a mixture of desire and devotion. Isabelle's hands slid up his chest, her fingers curling into his shirt as she leaned into him, her lips soft and warm against his.

Time seemed to stand still as they lost themselves in each other, their surroundings fading away until there was only the warmth of their embrace, the connection that ran deeper than anything he had ever known. Silas felt his love for her swelling inside him, filling every part of him with a fierce, consuming devotion. It was as though every moment they had ever shared, every look, every touch, had built to this, a love that defied everything even the darkness that threatened to consume them.

As he lifted her gently into his arms, he felt the weight of their shared journey, the struggles they had faced and the battles yet to come. He carried her through the mansion, their eyes locked, a silent promise passing between them a vow that whatever came their way, they would face it together. In her gaze, he saw a strength that mirrored his own, a determination that told him she was willing to stand by his side, no matter how dark the path became.

They reached his room, and he set her down carefully, his hand lingering on her cheek as he looked at her, the depth of his emotions laid bare. His gaze softened as he brushed a strand of hair from her face, his fingers lingering on her skin, memorizing every detail of her.

"You mean everything to me, Isabelle," he whispered, his voice filled with an intensity he could barely contain. "No matter what we face, no matter how dark things become... our love will survive. It's stronger than anything they can throw at us."

Isabelle's eyes shone with tears, and she smiled, her hand resting over his heart. "I believe that too, Silas," she murmured, her voice steady, filled with a quiet conviction. "Nothing can destroy what we have. Our love... it's eternal."

With those words, Silas's heart swelled, a newfound strength filling him, giving him the courage he needed to face whatever lay ahead. He kissed her again, slow and deep, pouring all of his love, his passion, into that kiss, as though he could shield her from the darkness with nothing but his devotion.

Chapter Seventeen

Illumination of the Heart

As the night wore on, Silas and Isabelle lay wrapped in each other's arms, their breaths slow and synchronized as they drifted in and out of a peaceful slumber. Silas's mind swirled with thoughts, lingering on the love he felt for her a love so deep it felt as though it transcended time itself. Soulmates. He'd heard the word spoken so many times across centuries by mortals, yet he'd never fully understood it until now. Isabelle was more than just his beloved; she was the missing piece of himself, the force that grounded him, even as shadows loomed on the horizon. She had brought him back from the edges of despair, and now, in her presence, he felt that perhaps even his curse was not something he faced alone.

His gaze softened as he watched her drift into sleep, her face relaxed, bathed in the soft glow of the moonlight streaming through the window. Every breath, every movement she made stirred something within him, a passion and devotion that went beyond mere mortal love. She was his light, his guide, the one who had somehow, impossibly, found her way to him across the vastness of time.

Isabelle stirred slightly, her thoughts slipping between dreams and wakefulness. Her love for Silas filled her completely, a warm, unbreakable bond that felt as though it had been written in her soul long before she had ever laid eyes on him. Soulmates. The word lingered in her mind, filled with both wonder and a quiet acceptance. She had always felt different, always sensed something within herself that she couldn't explain. And now, in Silas's arms, it was as though that missing part of herself had been filled, ignited by their love. She closed her eyes, the warmth of his embrace calming her, grounding her.

But as she lay against him, a strange, pulsing warmth began to build in her chest, a sensation unlike anything she had felt before. It started as a gentle glow, a flicker beneath her skin, and then it grew, filling her with a radiance that seemed to come from within her very heart. She felt the heat expand, reaching out, touching everything around her, until it became a soft, glowing light that illuminated the room.

Silas shifted slightly, feeling a sharp warmth against his skin where her chest rested against his. He winced, the sensation akin to a gentle burn, but he didn't pull away. Instead, he watched in amazement as the light radiated from Isabelle's heart, casting a gentle glow that bathed the room in a soft, ethereal light. The light was pure, almost blinding in its beauty, and as it touched him, he felt a strange sense of peace wash over him, as though every dark corner of his soul were being soothed by her presence.

Isabelle opened her eyes, confusion filling her gaze as she looked down at the glow emanating from her chest. "Silas..." she murmured, her voice trembling with both awe and fear. "What... what is this?"

Silas looked at her, his expression filled with wonder and concern. "I don't know," he whispered, his fingers gently brushing over the light as though afraid to break the moment. "But... it's coming from

you, Isabelle. It's as though there's something inside you, something...
powerful."

She touched her chest, feeling the warmth beneath her hand, her
mind spinning with questions. What is this? Where did this power
come from? And why now? She had never experienced anything like
this before, and the mystery of it filled her with both fascination and
unease. She couldn't shake the feeling that this light, this force within
her, was connected to something far greater than herself.

The next morning, Helena found them in the library, Isabelle's
hand resting lightly on her chest as she tried to process the strange
events of the night. Helena immediately noticed the confusion in her
expression, the uncertainty in her gaze.

"What's wrong?" Helena asked, her tone both curious and cautious
as she took a seat beside Isabelle.

Silas exchanged a glance with Isabelle, his expression filled with
both awe and concern. "Last night... something happened," he said
quietly, glancing at Isabelle as if to ask permission. When she nodded,
he continued, "There was a light, something glowing, coming from
her heart. It was... intense, powerful. But neither of us knows what it
means."

Helena's brow furrowed, a flicker of recognition sparking in her
gaze as she processed his words. "A light?" she repeated, her voice filled
with a mix of fascination and alarm. "From inside you, Isabelle?"

Isabelle nodded, her hand resting on her chest as though trying to
feel the remnants of the warmth that had been there only hours before.
"Yes. I don't know what it was, but it felt... like something I've never
felt before. Almost as if... it was a part of me that had been waiting."

Helena's expression grew serious, and she rose from her chair, moving toward one of the shelves where a set of old, leather-bound books
lay in neat rows. She scanned the spines carefully, her fingers tracing

over each title until she stopped, pulling a particular volume from the shelf. The book was ancient, its cover worn with age, and the title was barely legible in faded gold lettering: "The Celestial Chronicles."

Helena placed the book on the table, her fingers brushing over the cover with reverence. "I think I may have an idea of what's happening," she murmured, her gaze flicking to Isabelle. "This text is one of the oldest in the collection. It speaks of beings known as Celestials, guardians of light who walk among mortals, often unaware of their true nature until their powers are awakened by... something profound."

"Celestials?" Isabelle repeated, her voice filled with awe and disbelief. "I... I'm not sure I understand."

Helena opened the book, flipping through the yellowed pages until she reached a section filled with delicate, hand-painted illustrations of glowing figures, each one surrounded by an aura of light. She pointed to a passage, her voice filled with a mixture of reverence and excitement.

"Celestials are rare, born only once in several generations. They are beings of light, sent to the mortal realm to serve as protectors against forces that threaten to consume it," Helena explained, her eyes bright with wonder as she looked at Isabelle. "Their power lies dormant until it is ignited by something, usually a deep, powerful love or an act of pure devotion. I believe that your love for Silas, the connection you share, has awakened this dormant power within you."

Silas's gaze shifted to Isabelle, his heart pounding as he absorbed Helena's words. "So... Isabelle is a Celestial? A guardian of light?"

Helena nodded, her expression serious. "Yes. And this power, this light... it's not just any energy. It's a force meant to confront darkness, to combat ancient threats that would otherwise go unchecked." She looked at Isabelle, her gaze intense. "It's possible that your role in this battle against the old ones is more significant than we realized. You are not just a mortal caught in this conflict, Isabelle. You are a force that could help tip the scales."

Isabelle felt a surge of emotions wonder, confusion, fear all blending together in a whirl of thoughts that she could barely process. She had always sensed that she was different, but to learn that she was a Celestial, a guardian of light destined to face the darkness, was almost too much to comprehend. She looked at Silas, her heart pounding, a question lingering in her gaze.

"Silas... does this change things?" she whispered, her voice filled with uncertainty.

He took her hand, his gaze steady as he looked at her, the depth of his love and devotion shining in his eyes. "It only strengthens what I already knew, Isabelle," he murmured, his voice filled with quiet conviction. "Our love... it's not just something that happened. It's a bond that has existed across lifetimes, a force that has been waiting for this moment. Whatever darkness we face, we'll face it together. Your light, Isabelle... it only makes me love you more."

Isabelle felt a warmth spread through her chest, the glow from the night before flickering to life within her, filling her with a sense of purpose, a sense of destiny. She had been afraid, uncertain of what lay ahead, but now, with Silas by her side and the knowledge of her heritage guiding her, she felt a strength she had never known.

Helena closed the book, a solemn expression crossing her face as she looked at them both. "The road ahead will not be easy," she warned, her voice grave. "The old ones are powerful, and they will sense this light, this force within you, Isabelle. They will know that you are a threat. But if there is anyone who can face them... it's the two of you."

Silas and Isabelle exchanged a glance, a silent understanding passing between them. Their love, their connection, had awakened something that had lain dormant for centuries. They were no longer just two souls bound by fate; they were a force, a light that could stand against the darkness.

And as they held each other, a fierce determination filled them both. They knew that whatever awaited them, whatever shadows rose to challenge them, they would face it together.

For in the end, their love was more than just a bond. It was a promise, a promise that would endure through the darkness, a light that would guide them through even the darkest of nights.

Chapter Eighteen

Bound by Light and Shadow

The following morning dawned slowly, casting a soft, muted glow over the mansion. Silas sat at the edge of the bed, watching Isabelle as she slept peacefully beside him, her face relaxed, her chest rising and falling in a steady rhythm. The events of the night lingered in his mind, haunting him like an echo he couldn't shake. The memory of the light that had radiated from Isabelle's heart, warm and fierce, filled him with equal parts awe and apprehension. She was no ordinary mortal; she was a Celestial, a being of light born to face the darkness.

And while her power was only half-awakened, there was no denying the threat it could pose if fully unleashed.

He reached out, his fingers grazing her hand, careful not to disturb her. The warmth of her skin, so familiar, so grounding, reminded him why he had fought so hard to find her again, why he would fight for her still. But the memory of the slight burn he'd felt when the light had touched him nagged at him, a warning of the force within her. If her power were to awaken fully, the light of a Celestial could hurt him potentially even destroy him. The irony of it struck him deeply; the very thing that could vanquish the ancient darkness he sought to fight was the same thing that could separate them forever.

What does this mean for us? Silas thought, his mind racing with a mixture of emotions he could barely contain. How can I protect her from the world when her own power could keep her from me?

A heaviness settled over him as he looked at Isabelle, his love for her clashing with the fear that her newfound power might bring challenges he wasn't prepared to face. He had always considered himself a protector, a shield between her and the shadows that sought to consume them. But now, he felt an unfamiliar vulnerability, a realization that this power within her was beyond his control.

Isabelle could protect herself from forces far darker than I could defend her from. But what happens if that protection comes at the cost of our love?

Isabelle stirred, her eyes fluttering open as she looked up at him with a soft smile. "You're awake," she murmured, her voice drowsy but filled with warmth.

Silas forced a smile, reaching out to tuck a loose strand of hair behind her ear. "I couldn't sleep," he admitted, his voice low. "I've been thinking about... everything."

Isabelle's gaze softened, a look of understanding in her eyes. "The light..." she said quietly, her hand coming to rest over her heart. "I still don't understand what it means, why it's suddenly a part of me."

Silas nodded, his mind turning to Helena's words, the description of what it meant to be a Celestial, a being born from the essence of light, a guardian against ancient, destructive forces. They were rare, their powers often dormant until awakened by love, by devotion, by a passion so pure it ignited their very souls. Helena's description of a Celestial had been one of reverence and mystery, of a being who walked in both worlds, mortal and divine, who carried a light that could dispel darkness itself.

Celestials were timeless guardians, born in times of great need, destined to face shadows that threatened to consume the world. They were known only in whispered legends, protectors who operated unseen, their true identities hidden to keep them safe from those who would seek to destroy them. A Celestial's light was powerful, capable of banishing creatures born of darkness, but it was also dangerous. If fully ignited, the light could harm any dark creature it touched, friend or foe.

Silas's heart tightened at the thought. If Isabelle's power were to awaken fully, it could drive away not just their enemies, but himself as well. The realization stung, filling him with a deep, aching sadness. Isabelle was everything to him, his soulmate, his anchor in a world of shadows, but now her light presented a danger he hadn't anticipated.

Isabelle seemed to sense his hesitation, her expression growing concerned as she looked at him. "Silas... what is it?" she asked softly, her hand finding his, her touch gentle and grounding.

He took a deep breath, his fingers closing around hers. "Isabelle," he began, his voice barely above a whisper. "Your light... it's powerful. More powerful than we realized. If it were to fully awaken..." He hesitated, searching for the right words, not wanting to frighten her. "It could... harm me. Maybe even destroy me."

Her eyes widened, a mixture of horror and disbelief flashing across her face. "No," she whispered, shaking her head. "I would never want to hurt you, Silas. You're—" She paused, her voice catching. "You're everything to me."

He pulled her close, wrapping his arms around her, his lips brushing against her forehead as he held her. "I know," he murmured, his voice filled with a fierce determination. "And I will do everything I can to protect you, to keep us safe. But there are forces out there ancient forces that will see you as a threat. If they discover who you are, they will come for you."

A sense of dread settled over her, the reality of her new identity sinking in. "What do we do?" she asked, her voice barely a whisper.

Silas's gaze hardened, a spark of determination flickering in his eyes. "We keep this hidden," he said firmly. "We tell no one. If the old ones, or any of their followers, discover that a Celestial walks among them, they will stop at nothing to find you, to destroy you before your power can fully awaken. For now, we keep this between us, and Helena."

Isabelle nodded, her expression filled with a mixture of fear and resolve. She hadn't asked for this power, this heritage, but she could feel the weight of it, the responsibility that came with it. She had always known she was different, always felt a strange connection to forces she couldn't explain. But now, with her love for Silas awakening her powers, she understood that this was her purpose, her destiny.

As they sat together in the quiet of the room, Isabelle's mind drifted back to the strange glow that had emanated from her heart. It had felt foreign yet familiar, as though it had been a part of her all along, lying dormant until her love for Silas had ignited it. But now, with that light awakened, she could feel a pull, a silent call urging her to protect, to defend, to face the darkness that threatened to consume them.

In the quiet of the morning, Helena entered, her eyes solemn as she carried an old, leather-bound book in her arms. She looked at them both, her expression grave as she set the book down on the table between them. "I found this in the archives," she said, her voice barely above a whisper. "It's an ancient text, one that speaks of Celestials and their purpose. I believe it may hold the answers we're looking for."

Silas's gaze shifted to the book, his fingers tracing over the worn cover. The title was faint, barely visible, but he could make out the words in an archaic script: "The Celestial Doctrine." The book was filled with hand-drawn symbols and descriptions, detailing the nature of Celestials, their powers, and the dangers they faced.

Helena opened the book to a marked page, her finger pointing to a passage written in dark, flowing script. "It says here that Celestials are born in times of great darkness, their light a force meant to counterbalance the shadows that seek to consume the world. They are protectors, guardians of life and hope, but their power is as much a curse as it is a gift. A Celestial's light can repel any dark creature, friend or foe, and if fully ignited, their power can destroy even those they hold dear."

Silas's chest tightened at the words, the weight of their meaning settling over him. Isabelle's power was not just a weapon against the old ones; it was a force that could drive him away, that could tear them apart.

Helena looked at Isabelle, her gaze filled with both awe and concern. "You are not just a mortal caught in this war, Isabelle. You are a Celestial, a guardian meant to face the darkness. But you must be careful. If the old ones, or their followers, discover your identity, they will come for you. And if your power fully awakens, it could—"

"I know," Isabelle interrupted softly, her voice steady despite the fear that lingered in her gaze. "I understand the risks, Helena. But I can't turn away from this. If my light can protect those I love, then I'll do whatever it takes to harness it."

Silas reached for her hand, his gaze filled with a fierce determination. "We'll face this together," he said firmly. "I won't let them take you. I won't let anything come between us."

A quiet resolve settled over them, a silent understanding that bound them together even more tightly than before. They would face the darkness, the dangers that awaited them, and they would do so side by side, bound by a love that transcended even the ancient forces that threatened to tear them apart.

And as they sat together, the weight of their destinies looming over them, they knew that whatever the future held, their love would be their guiding light, a beacon in the darkness, a force that no shadow could extinguish.

CHAPTER NINETEEN

SHADOWS OF THE PAST

As the day slipped into twilight, Silas paced the length of his study, his mind churning with thoughts of Isabelle's newfound power. The revelation of her Celestial heritage was as awe-inspiring as it was terrifying. Silas had always known that his life came with risks, with enemies lurking in the dark, but Isabelle's light had raised the stakes in ways he hadn't anticipated. If the old ones or any of their followers discovered her true nature, they would stop at nothing to eliminate her before she could stand against them.

He clenched his fists, the weight of his helplessness gnawing at him. He had to protected Isabelle through countless dangers, and now he faced the bitter reality that her own light the very essence of who she was might drive them apart.

He needed guidance, counsel from someone who understood the world beyond his own knowledge. And there was only one person he could trust with such a delicate matter: Ronan.

Silas had known Ronan for centuries, and despite the mysteries surrounding him, their bond had always been one of loyalty and mutual respect. Ronan was one of the few vampires Silas truly trusted, a friend who had been a part of his life during some of its darkest chapters. But Ronan had vanished long ago, slipping into the shadows, hiding from the world in a way that few vampires could. Rumors circulated among their kind, whispers of a powerful vampire who had turned his back on the immortal life, hiding in obscurity to evade both allies and enemies.

So why has he come back now? Silas wondered, his mind filled with questions and doubts. The answer that lingered at the edge of his thoughts filled him with both hope and fear: perhaps Ronan had returned because he sensed the presence of a Celestial.

As the sun dipped below the horizon, Silas slipped out of the mansion and made his way to a secluded spot on the outskirts of the city, where the darkness lay thick and heavy, untouched by the lights of New York. He waited in the silence, his senses alert, every shadow a potential danger. He had reached out to Ronan telepathically, sending a message that only a trusted friend would answer. If Ronan was still the man Silas remembered, he would come under the cover of night, unseen by the mortal world.

Moments later, a figure emerged from the darkness, moving with the kind of silent grace that only centuries of experience could cultivate. Silas's breath caught as he recognized the tall, lean figure of Ronan, his dark hair falling to his shoulders, his eyes sharp and intense, even in the dim light.

"Silas," Ronan greeted, his voice soft but edged with a quiet strength. "It's been too long."

Silas nodded, a flood of emotions rushing through him. Relief, gratitude, and a lingering unease filled him as he took in the sight of his old friend. Ronan looked much the same as he remembered, though there was a new hardness in his eyes, a wariness that suggested he had not come without his own burdens.

"Thank you for coming," Silas said, his voice filled with genuine relief. "I wasn't sure if you would answer."

Ronan's gaze softened slightly, a faint smile touching his lips. "For you, Silas, I would always answer. But I must admit, your message surprised me. You know I've kept myself hidden for a reason."

Silas studied him, his mind filled with questions he had held onto for years. "Where have you been, Ronan? You vanished without a trace, and no one has seen or heard from you in centuries."

Ronan's expression grew somber, his eyes drifting to the dark horizon. "I've been hiding," he admitted, his voice barely above a whisper. "Avoiding both allies and enemies, keeping my existence a secret. The world has changed, Silas, and our kind is more divided than ever. I chose to disappear to avoid the dangers that came with my name, to protect myself from those who would use my power for their own ends."

Silas nodded, understanding the weight of his friend's decision. The life of a vampire was fraught with rivalries and alliances, each as treacherous as the last. And Ronan's reputation, his strength, made him a target for those who would seek to control or destroy him.

"But why now?" Silas pressed, his gaze searching Ronan's face. "Why return after all this time? What made you step out of the shadows?"

Ronan hesitated, his expression guarded as though weighing his words carefully. "I returned because I sensed… something. A presence I haven't felt in centuries. A force that could disrupt the balance of the world as we know it." He looked directly at Silas, his eyes filled with a quiet intensity. "I came back because I believe a Celestial walks among us."

Silas felt a chill run through him, confirming his suspicions. Ronan's return wasn't a coincidence; he had come back because of Isabelle. Somehow, her light had called to him, drawing him out of hiding, pulling him back into a world he had long since abandoned.

"I was right, wasn't I?" Ronan asked, his voice low. "There is a Celestial here, in New York."

Silas hesitated, his instincts urging him to protect Isabelle, to keep her existence a secret. But Ronan's gaze held an unwavering trust, a reminder of the loyalty they had shared through centuries. Silas nodded slowly, his voice barely a whisper. "Yes... there is."

Ronan's expression shifted, a mixture of awe and concern flickering across his face. "Then you understand the danger she's in. If the old ones, or any of their followers, discover her existence, they will come for her. A Celestial's light is a threat to them, a force that can banish them to oblivion. She is their greatest weakness."

Silas's jaw tightened, his chest filled with a fierce, protective rage. "I know," he said, his voice laced with determination. "And that's why I need your help, Ronan. I can't protect her alone. Not against forces like these."

Ronan nodded, his gaze steady. "I'll stand by you, Silas. But you must understand... if I'm discovered, it could bring even greater danger. I've avoided our kind for centuries, keeping myself hidden from those who would hunt me down. If my presence becomes known, it could draw the attention of not just the old ones, but others who would seek to use Isabelle's power for their own ends."

"Where have you been hiding all these years?" Silas asked, his curiosity getting the better of him.

Ronan's gaze shifted, his expression distant as he remembered the years he had spent in isolation. "I've traveled to places our kind would never think to look. I stayed in the mountains of Tibet, living among monks who saw me as nothing more than a wandering spirit. I sought refuge in the deserts of the Middle East, hiding in ruins untouched for centuries. I even journeyed to the edges of the Arctic, where I could exist in silence, far from the reach of anyone who would try to find me." He looked back at Silas, a faint sadness in his eyes. "I've been a ghost, Silas, a shadow of my former self. But I returned because of her. Because I knew a Celestial would soon awaken, and that I was needed."

Silas's heart ached at the thought of his friend's solitude, the sacrifices Ronan had made to protect himself from the very world they once knew. And now, here he was, stepping back into danger for the sake of a Celestial he hadn't even met. Silas knew that his trust in Ronan was well placed, that his friend would stand by him even in the face of the ancient dangers that awaited them.

"Thank you," Silas said quietly, his voice filled with gratitude. "Your help means more than you know."

Ronan's gaze softened, his expression filled with a quiet determination. "I'm here, Silas. And I'll stay as long as you need me. But we must be cautious. The old ones have followers everywhere, allies who would give anything to gain favor with them. If they suspect there is a Celestial among us, they will stop at nothing to find her."

Silas nodded, his mind filled with thoughts of Isabelle, her face, her light, the fierce determination in her gaze. She was more than just a Celestial to him; she was the love of his life, the one person who had given him purpose in the darkness. And he would protect her, no matter the cost.

"We'll be careful," Silas said, his voice filled with a quiet resolve. "We'll keep her power hidden, at least until we're ready to confront the old ones. And when that time comes... we'll face them together."

Ronan placed a hand on Silas's shoulder, a silent vow of loyalty passing between them. "Until then, I'll be watching," he said softly.

"If you need me, I'll be here. But be vigilant, Silas. There are forces at play that we don't fully understand. And if the old ones discover her existence... they will stop at nothing to destroy her."

With a final nod, Ronan stepped back, his figure blending into the shadows, disappearing as silently as he had arrived. Silas watched him go, a mixture of gratitude and apprehension settling over him. He knew that their journey was only beginning, that the road ahead would be fraught with danger and darkness. But with Ronan by his side, and Isabelle's light to guide him, he felt a renewed sense of purpose, a strength that would carry him through whatever lay ahead.

As he turned back toward the mansion, his heart filled with a fierce determination. They would face the darkness together, and no force, not even the old ones, would keep him from protecting the woman he loved.

Chapter Twenty

Whispers of Secrets

Silas made his way back to the mansion, his footsteps echoing softly against the empty streets, each step carrying the weight of his troubled thoughts. Despite the solace he'd found in Ronan's reappearance, a gnawing sense of unease lingered in his mind. Something about their conversation felt incomplete, as though Ronan had been holding back, wrestling with words he couldn't bring himself to say. Silas couldn't shake the feeling that his old friend had hidden something, something crucial, something that perhaps involved Isabelle.

How much does he know? Silas wondered, his heart heavy with an ache he couldn't explain. Ronan's return had rekindled memories he'd tried to bury, memories of battles they had fought together, of the trust they'd built over centuries. And yet, there had always been a part of Ronan that was veiled, a mystery Silas had accepted, believing that Ronan's secrets were his own to keep. But now, that secrecy felt like a shadow cast over their friendship, a reminder that even the closest bonds had their limits.

As he reached the mansion, Silas paused, casting one last glance over his shoulder, half-expecting to see Ronan's figure lingering in the shadows. But the night was silent, empty, as if Ronan had never been there at all. Silas felt a pang of longing a desire to understand, to know the depths of the journey his friend had endured in solitude. The centuries Ronan had spent in isolation, evading both allies and enemies, had changed him. There was a hardness in Ronan's gaze, a distance that Silas couldn't ignore. But there was also something else an unspoken fear, a caution that hinted at knowledge too dark to share.

Silas closed his eyes, drawing a slow breath to steady himself. What are you hiding, Ronan? What burden do you carry that you can't share, even with me?

The question burned within him, twisting his insides with a mixture of anger and concern. He could still feel the hesitation in Ronan's voice, the subtle shift in his expression as he spoke of Isabelle's power, of the dangers that awaited them. There had been something unsaid, a flicker of unease that had passed through Ronan's eyes, as if he knew more than he was willing to admit.

She's in more danger than you're telling me, Silas thought bitterly, his hands clenching at his sides. You sensed something… but you won't tell me what it is.

He knew that pressing Ronan for answers would only drive his friend further into secrecy, but the thought of Isabelle being caught in the crossfire of an ancient war made his blood run cold. She was everything to him, his light in a world of shadows, and the idea that Ronan might be hiding something that concerned her filled him with a fury he could barely contain.

As he pushed open the door to the mansion, Silas's mind was a storm of emotions, anger, worry, frustration, and a deep sense of betrayal. He had trusted Ronan, believed in their bond, but now he was beginning to question that trust. He couldn't shake the feeling that his friend had returned not just to help him, but for another purpose one that he wasn't ready to reveal.

So many years lost, Silas thought, his heart aching with the weight of the time that had slipped away. Ronan's absence had been a wound he'd carried for centuries, a reminder of the loneliness that came with immortality. And now, just when he needed his friend the most, it felt as though Ronan was still holding back, still keeping him at arm's length.

He made his way through the quiet halls of the mansion, his thoughts returning to the last time he had seen Ronan, centuries ago, before his friend had vanished into the shadows. They had fought side by side, their trust forged in the heat of battle, each one knowing that the other would protect him without question. But then Ronan had disappeared, leaving nothing but whispers and rumors in his wake. Silas had searched for him, tried to trace his path, but Ronan had covered his tracks too well. And eventually, Silas had accepted his friend's absence, burying the pain, the questions, the betrayal.

And now, here he was, returned under the cover of darkness, carrying secrets he couldn't.....or wouldn't share.

So why come back at all? Silas wondered, his heart pounding as he grappled with the conflicting emotions that warred within him. What is it about Isabelle that drew you out of hiding? What do you know that you won't tell me?

As he climbed the stairs to his room, Silas's thoughts drifted to Isabelle, to the light that had radiated from her heart, the power that had lain dormant within her for so long. He knew now that her existence was both a blessing and a curse, a force that could save them all, but one that also painted a target on her back. Her Celestial nature was a rare, beautiful gift, but it came with dangers he hadn't foreseen, dangers that even Ronan seemed unwilling to fully acknowledge.

He reached his room, closing the door behind him as he sat down on the edge of the bed, his head in his hands. The weight of the night pressed down on him, and for the first time in centuries, he felt truly powerless. He had always prided himself on his strength, his ability to protect those he cared for, but now, with Isabelle's life hanging in the balance, he felt like a man standing on the edge of a cliff, unable to see what lay below.

The silence was broken by a soft knock at the door, and he looked up, his heart pounding as Isabelle entered, her face filled with concern.

"Silas?" she said softly, moving to sit beside him. "Are you all right? You've been so quiet since you returned."

Silas forced a smile, reaching out to take her hand, his thumb tracing gentle circles over her skin. "I'm... fine," he murmured, though he could hear the hollowness in his own voice. "It's just... there's so much happening, so much I didn't anticipate."

Isabelle's gaze softened, and she leaned against him, her head resting on his shoulder. "You don't have to carry this alone, you know. Whatever dangers we face, we'll face them together."

Her words brought a bittersweet comfort, a reminder of the strength they shared, but Silas couldn't shake the feeling that he was failing her, that he was somehow missing a crucial piece of the puzzle. Ronan's return had stirred up more questions than answers, and his friend's reluctance to fully disclose his knowledge left a bitter taste in his mouth.

"I just... I worry," Silas admitted, his voice barely above a whisper. "I worry that there's more to this than we realize, that we're being drawn into a game we don't fully understand."

Isabelle placed a hand on his chest, her gaze filled with a quiet determination. "Whatever it is, whatever comes our way, we'll face it. I trust you, Silas. And I trust in our love. That's something no force, not even the old ones, can take from us."

Her words stirred something within him, a spark of hope that cut through the darkness. He wrapped his arms around her, pulling her close as he rested his chin on her head, savoring the warmth of her embrace, the steady beat of her heart. She was his light, his reason for fighting, and he would do whatever it took to protect her, to keep her safe from the shadows that sought to consume them.

But even as he held her, a lingering unease gnawed at him, a fear that whispered in the back of his mind. There was more to this, more to Ronan's return, and he couldn't shake the feeling that his friend's silence hid a truth he wasn't ready to face.

As he drifted into a restless sleep, Ronan's parting words echoed in his mind, a reminder of the dangers that lay ahead:

"Be careful, my friend. There are forces at play that we cannot fully understand. And they will stop at nothing to destroy everything you hold dear."

And with that, Silas knew that their journey was only beginning, that the darkness lurking in the shadows was far deeper, far older, than he had ever imagined.

Chapter Twenty-One

Shadows in the Stacks

Silas's mind churned with an intensity he couldn't quell. Ever since Ronan had reappeared, stirring memories of the life they'd once shared and secrets that stretched back centuries, Silas had been unable to shake the feeling that his friend was hiding something, something that concerned Isabelle. The more he tried to piece together Ronan's cryptic warnings, the deeper he felt himself falling into a darkness that threatened to consume him. The weight of his responsibilities bore down on him, each new discovery twisting his thoughts, pushing him to places he had not ventured in years.

So many questions, and still, no answers.

His frustration simmered, each attempt to trace the old ones proving fruitless. They had evaded him, as if they were mere ghosts, lingering in the shadows, leaving behind only whispers and rumors. Every lead he'd followed had ended in dead silence, each source too afraid to speak of them or, worse, denying their existence entirely. They were elusive, always one step ahead, and as the days wore on, Silas felt the noose tightening. He was running out of time, and he couldn't shake the feeling that something was closing in around them.

In the quiet of the mansion, he sat alone, his thoughts growing darker with each passing hour. Ronan's reluctance, his evasive answers, filled him with suspicion. What could he possibly fear so much that he couldn't tell me? Why come back after all this time, only to leave me with riddles?

And Isabelle... Isabelle was at the center of it all, her Celestial power a beacon that had somehow drawn both Ronan and the threat of the old ones. Her light was beautiful, a force of hope and love, but it also painted a target on her back a target he could feel lurking closer with each passing day.

Meanwhile, across town, Helena moved quickly through the dimly lit corridors of the New York Public Library. She had always known the library's halls and shelves well, her love for ancient texts and forgotten knowledge guiding her many late-night research trips. Tonight, however, her mission was different. She had felt the weight of Silas's desperation, the sense of urgency in his voice as they had discussed the mysteries surrounding Isabelle's powers and the looming threat of the old ones. Silas's frustration had been palpable, and Helena was determined to find any information that might help him.

As the clock struck midnight, she was alone, the vast expanse of the library quiet and dim. Her contact, a friend in the archives, had agreed to give her after-hours access, trusting in Helena's discretion and her passion for ancient mysteries. It had been years since she had explored the deep storage areas of the library, and as she descended the narrow staircase to the lower floors, she couldn't shake the feeling that something significant awaited her in the dark recesses of the archives.

The basement storage room was vast and filled with towering shelves, each stacked with books and documents too fragile or obscure for the main library. Dust floated in the air, illuminated by the faint glow of her lantern as she moved slowly, her fingers trailing along the spines of ancient tomes, each one a relic of a different age.

And then, at the very back of the room, buried beneath a pile of old manuscripts, she saw it a book that called to her with a strange pull, its spine worn and cracked, the leather cover aged to a deep, mottled brown. She pulled it free, her heart racing as she examined it. The title, faded but still legible, sent a chill through her:

"The Chronicles of the Forgotten Ones."

The words were written in a script that was both haunting and beautiful, each letter curling and twisting in a way that seemed almost alive. Helena's hands trembled as she opened the book, her eyes scanning the fragile pages, each one filled with ancient script and illustrations that depicted creatures she had only heard of in legends.

As she turned the pages, she felt a sense of relief and awe. This was what they had been searching for the answers to the questions that had plagued Silas and threatened Isabelle. The book described the old ones in detail, their origins, their powers, and, most importantly, their weaknesses. The text spoke of the Celestials as well, their role as protectors, their power to dispel darkness a force feared by the old ones, a power that had the potential to destroy them.

But as she read further, a feeling of dread settled over her. The book warned of the dangers to the Celestials themselves, the sacrifices they would have to make, the pain they would endure. It described the ancient struggle between light and dark, a battle that was older than time itself, a battle that Isabelle was now fated to fight.

Helena's heart raced as she took in the enormity of the task before them. She closed the book, clutching it tightly as she turned to leave. Relief mingled with fear, a sense of urgency pushing her to return to the mansion as quickly as possible.

As she made her way back through the empty halls of the library, a sudden chill ran down her spine. She paused, glancing over her shoulder, her instincts prickling with the awareness that she was no longer alone. The shadows seemed to shift, dark shapes moving at the edges of her vision, and a sense of unease settled over her.

Helena quickened her pace, her fingers tightening around the book as she reached the main floor, her footsteps echoing loudly in the empty space. She could feel it now, a presence following her, lurking in the shadows, watching her with a malevolent intent. She didn't dare look back, her heart pounding as she pushed open the heavy doors and stepped out into the night.

The city streets were quiet, the streetlamps casting pools of light onto the cobblestone pavement. Helena kept moving, her senses heightened, every instinct urging her to run. She could feel the presence behind her, closing in, and a surge of fear shot through her as she realized she had nowhere to go, no place to hide.

But then, as she turned a corner, she felt a shift in the air, a strange warmth flooding over her, and in her mind, she saw him, Silas. His face appeared before her, his eyes filled with concern, his voice a whisper in her mind:

"Helena... you're not alone. I'm coming."

The vision faded, but the connection remained, a lifeline that steadied her, gave her the strength to keep moving. She could feel Silas's presence, his determination, his protective spirit reaching out to her, and it filled her with a sense of hope.

In a nearby alley, Silas appeared out of the shadows, his figure sharp and imposing as he scanned the streets, his gaze intense as he searched for her. Helena let out a breath of relief, her footsteps quickening as she moved toward him, her heart pounding with both fear and gratitude.

Just as she reached him, a dark figure emerged from the shadows, a vampire whose eyes gleamed with a cold, predatory hunger. Silas's expression hardened, his stance shifting as he stepped in front of Helena, shielding her from the threat.

The vampire sneered, his gaze flicking between Silas and Helena, a twisted smile playing on his lips. "You think you can hide her, Silas?" he taunted, his voice dripping with malice. "The old ones know. They're watching, waiting. She won't escape them."

Silas's jaw clenched, his gaze cold and unyielding. "Then let them come," he replied, his voice a low, dangerous growl. "But know this, you won't be the one to deliver her to them."

With a swift, fluid motion, Silas lunged at the vampire, his movements precise and deadly. The two clashed in a flurry of strikes, each blow echoing through the empty streets as they fought, shadows and light intertwining in a deadly dance.

Helena watched, her heart racing as Silas overpowered the vampire, his strength and skill unmatched. Within moments, the vampire lay motionless, his form dissolving into ashes that scattered in the wind.

Silas turned to her, his gaze softening as he took in her disheveled appearance, the fear that lingered in her eyes. He stepped forward, his hand reaching out to touch her shoulder, grounding her, reminding her that she was safe.

"Helena," he murmured, his voice filled with concern. "Are you all right?"

She nodded, her hand clutching the ancient book as she met his gaze. "I found it, Silas," she whispered, her voice trembling with relief. "The book... it holds the answers we've been searching for. It describes the old ones, their weaknesses, their fears. And it speaks of the Celestials... of Isabelle's role in this."

Silas's expression shifted, a mixture of relief and determination filling his gaze. "Then we're one step closer," he said softly, his hand squeezing her shoulder in gratitude. "Thank you, Helena. I don't know what we would do without you."

A faint smile touched her lips, and she looked down at the book, the weight of its secrets pressing down on her. "There's much more to uncover, Silas. But I believe this is the key to understanding Isabelle's power... and the threat we're up against."

Silas nodded, his gaze filled with a fierce determination as he looked toward the horizon, the shadows of the night stretching before them. The road ahead was treacherous, filled with dangers he could barely comprehend, but he knew one thing for certain he would protect Isabelle, no matter the cost.

And as he led Helena back to the mansion, his mind was filled with thoughts of the old ones, of the secrets that lay within the ancient book, and of the woman he loved, whose light had become both his greatest hope and his deepest fear.

Chapter Twenty-Two

Shadows of Knowledge

The city lay quiet as Silas and Helena made their way back to the mansion, but the silence was deceptive, a shroud that barely concealed the tension simmering beneath it. Every corner, every shadow seemed to shift as though alive, and Silas's senses were heightened, his mind filled with questions and fears that he couldn't shake. Beside him, Helena clutched the ancient book, her fingers tight around its cover as though it alone held the key to their survival. Both of them were wrapped in a tense silence, their thoughts heavy, words unsaid hovering between them like ghosts.

As they walked, Silas's mind raced, the weight of his responsibilities pressing down on him. He glanced at Helena, catching the flicker of unease in her eyes, and he felt a pang of guilt that she, too, was drawn into this struggle. If it weren't for me, would she be in danger right now? he wondered, his mind filled with questions that had no answers.

The streets felt darker than usual, the shadows stretching long and deep, and Silas could see figures darting just beyond his line of sight, their movements swift and silent, like creatures of the night drawn by some unspoken call. He felt a chill run down his spine, a warning that whatever threat they faced was closer than ever. He tightened his grip on Helena's shoulder, his gaze shifting constantly, watching, waiting.

"Silas," Helena whispered, her voice barely audible, her eyes darting nervously to the shadows around them. "Do you feel it? We're being watched."

Silas nodded, his voice low and steady. "Yes. But keep walking. We'll talk about this when we're safe inside the mansion."

Helena swallowed hard, but she kept pace with him, her mind racing as she clutched the book tighter, her thoughts a swirl of fear and determination. The ancient tome she held was their only link to understanding Isabelle's role in this looming war, and its worn, cracked leather cover held secrets that terrified and fascinated her in equal measure. She had glimpsed only a fraction of the text, but even that had revealed a history so dark, so ancient, that it sent shivers down her spine.

The Chronicles of the Forgotten Ones. The title alone hinted at truths that had been buried for millennia, stories of creatures older than time itself, beings that lurked in the darkest corners of the world. The book spoke of the old ones in haunting detail, describing their rise, their fall, and the centuries of slumber that had followed. But it was the passages about the Celestials that had struck her the most, each word a reminder of the role Isabelle was fated to play, the battle she would soon face.

Helena, she told herself, if this is true, then Isabelle's power isn't just a gift it's a burden, one that could consume her.

Beside her, Silas's thoughts mirrored her own, his mind clouded with memories of his brief conversation with Ronan and the lingering suspicion that his friend had withheld crucial information. The weight of Isabelle's destiny pressed down on him, a force he couldn't protect her from, not in the way he wanted to. She was a Celestial, her light a beacon that would draw enemies from every corner of the darkness, and no matter how fiercely he fought, he knew that he couldn't shield her from the dangers that awaited her.

As much as I want to protect her, I can't take away her fate, he thought bitterly, a helplessness twisting inside him. Her light, her power... it's as much a part of her as the air she breathes. But how can I let her face this alone?

As they walked, Silas noticed shadows flitting in the periphery, their movements too quick, too elusive to follow. His grip on Helena's shoulder tightened, his gaze scanning their surroundings, his senses alert. "Stay close," he murmured, his voice low. "We're almost there."

Helena nodded, her heart pounding as they turned the corner that led to the mansion. The familiar structure loomed ahead, its darkened windows and stone facade a stark contrast to the warmth within. Relief washed over her, but her mind remained uneasy, her thoughts returning to the book and the words that had haunted her since she had first opened its pages.

They slipped inside, the mansion's heavy door closing behind them with a solid thud, and for a moment, silence filled the entryway, a brief, fragile reprieve. Helena felt her shoulders relax slightly, the tension draining from her body as she looked at Silas, the weight of everything they had learned evident in his expression.

He gestured toward the drawing room, his gaze dark. "We'll talk in there," he said, his voice steady but tense. "No one else needs to hear this. Not yet."

Helena followed him into the room, her mind spinning with the knowledge she had uncovered, the secrets that now lay heavy on her heart. She placed the book on the table between them, her fingers lingering on its cover, as though reluctant to let go. Silas watched her, his expression unreadable, but she could sense the fear, the worry that simmered beneath the surface.

Finally, she looked up, meeting his gaze. "This book," she began, her voice barely above a whisper, "it's more than just a record of history. It's... it's a warning."

Silas's eyes narrowed, his jaw tightening as he listened. "A warning?"

Helena nodded, her fingers tracing the ancient script on the book's cover. "The Chronicles of the Forgotten Ones, it speaks of a time when the old ones ruled, when darkness held sway over the world. But it also tells of a prophecy, a time when a Celestial would rise, a being of light who could challenge them, drive them back into the shadows." She paused, her voice trembling slightly. "The Celestial isn't just a guardian, Silas. She's their destruction."

Silas's heart pounded at her words, the reality of Isabelle's role settling over him like a dark cloud. Isabelle wasn't just a protector; she was a threat, a force that the old ones would stop at nothing to eliminate. And the more her power grew, the more dangerous her presence would become.

Helena continued, her voice low. "The book also describes the dangers a Celestial faces the enemies they attract, the sacrifices they must make. It mentions..." She hesitated, her gaze drifting to the floor. "It mentions that a Celestial's power can be... consuming. That their light, if unchecked, can destroy not only the darkness, but everything around them. Friends, allies..." Her voice trailed off, and she looked at Silas, a shadow of fear in her eyes.

Silas clenched his fists, a wave of anger and helplessness washing over him. "So, her light... her very essence, is both a gift and a curse," he murmured, his voice laced with bitterness. "And there's nothing I can do to protect her from it."

Helena shook her head, her expression somber. "I don't know, Silas. The book speaks of a ritual, a way to channel a Celestial's power, to help them control it. But the details are... vague, and there are warnings, dangers that we don't fully understand."

Silas's gaze drifted to the book, his mind filled with thoughts of Isabelle, the woman he loved, and the impossible destiny she now faced. She was his light, his anchor in the darkness, but her power was a force he couldn't control, a weapon that could destroy her as easily as it could save them.

"What else did you find?" he asked, his voice a mixture of desperation and determination.

Helena flipped through the pages, her fingers trembling slightly as she scanned the text. "The old ones... they have weaknesses, vulnerabilities that we may be able to exploit. But their power is... vast, and their followers are everywhere. They're patient, Silas, willing to wait for centuries if it means securing their victory."

Silas's jaw tightened, a sense of dread settling over him. So we're fighting an enemy that's nearly invincible, and the only weapon we have is a power that could destroy us all. The thought filled him with a dark, simmering anger, a frustration that clawed at him, leaving him feeling helpless in the face of a threat he couldn't defeat.

As he sat there, his mind a storm of conflicting emotions, he caught sight of movement in the corner of the room, a flicker of shadow that darted across the wall, vanishing before he could fully register it. He tensed, his gaze sharpening as he rose from his seat, his senses alert.

"Helena," he said quietly, his voice filled with a tense urgency. "We're not alone."

Helena's eyes widened, her hand reaching instinctively for the book as she glanced around the room, her heart pounding. "Do you think... they followed us?"

Silas's gaze darkened, his voice a low, dangerous whisper. "I don't think. I know."

They exchanged a glance, a silent understanding passing between them, and Silas's resolve hardened. The shadows were closing in around them, the threat of the old ones growing with each passing day. But he would fight, he would protect Isabelle, no matter the cost.

And as they stood together in the dimly lit room, the ancient book lying between them, Silas made a silent vow, a promise that no matter what dangers awaited them, he would face them with unyielding strength, with the love he carried for Isabelle guiding him through the darkness.

Chapter Twenty-Three

The Haunting Shadows

The soft glow of the candlelight flickered against the pages of The Chronicles of the Forgotten Ones, casting eerie shadows on the walls of the drawing room. Silas sat at the edge of his chair, his eyes scanning the delicate, aged script with an intensity that seemed to burn. Helena sat across from him, the ancient tome spread open on the table between them, her fingers gently tracing the symbols etched into the margins.

Both of them were consumed by the weight of the text. The book's words, though faded, carried a dark gravity, a sense of foreboding that made each sentence feel heavier than the last.

Silas's mind was a storm. The revelations within the book stirred a fierce anger and a deeper frustration. So many warnings, so many cryptic passages. Why can't there be clear answers? His thoughts spiraled as he reread a passage about the old ones' followers, creatures bound to their will, who existed to ensure their return. The description was maddeningly vague, referring to these beings as "shadows given form" and speaking of their ability to stalk their prey from the edges of perception.

He clenched his fists, his nails digging into his palms as his agitation grew. The flickering of the shadows outside the mansion's windows didn't help. They danced and twisted, flitting just beyond the range of light, their movements almost playful yet filled with malice. They had followed Helena and the book back to the mansion, lingering, taunting, as though daring Silas to act.

Helena, too, felt the weight of the situation pressing down on her, though she fought to keep her emotions in check. Her gaze shifted from the book to Silas, watching the tension in his shoulders, the way his jaw tightened each time the shadows darted into view. She could feel the energy in the room, taut and electric, as if Silas himself were a storm waiting to break.

"I don't understand," Silas said, his voice low and rough. He gestured to the passage before him, frustration clear in his tone. "Why speak in riddles? 'Shadows given form.' What does that even mean? Are they physical beings? Illusions? How do we fight something we can't even define?"

Helena frowned, her own frustration bubbling beneath the surface. "I think that's the point," she replied, her voice steady despite the fear gnawing at her. "They want us confused, afraid. The less we understand, the more power they hold over us."

Her words were logical, but they did little to soothe Silas. He stood abruptly, pacing the room as the shadows outside grew bolder, their movements faster, more deliberate. He could hear faint whispers now, soft and mocking, words he couldn't quite make out but which grated against his nerves like nails on glass.

"Do you hear that?" Silas asked sharply, turning to Helena.

She nodded, her expression grim. "Yes. They're trying to get inside your head."

Silas's eyes narrowed, his frustration boiling over. He moved toward the window, his fists clenched, his gaze locked on the twisting darkness just beyond the glass. "Enough of this," he growled. "I won't sit here and let them toy with us. If they want a fight, I'll give them one."

"Silas, stop!" Helena's voice cut through his rising anger, sharp and commanding. She stood, placing herself between him and the window, her hands raised to block his path. "This is exactly what they want you to do."

Silas's eyes flashed with anger, but Helena didn't flinch. She met his gaze with an intensity that matched his own, her voice firm as she continued. "Think, Silas. You're stronger than they are, yes, but they're not trying to defeat you. They're trying to distract you, to draw you out. And while you're out there fighting them, they'll come in here. They'll go for Isabelle. Is that what you want?"

Her words hit him like a blow, and Silas froze, his anger giving way to a cold realization. His mind raced as he pictured Isabelle, vulnerable and unaware, asleep upstairs while the shadows plotted their way inside. The thought of losing her, of failing to protect her, sent a shiver of dread through him.

He closed his eyes, drawing a shaky breath as he stepped back, his fists relaxing at his sides. "You're right," he said hoarsely, his voice heavy with guilt. "You're right. I wasn't thinking."

Helena placed a reassuring hand on his arm, her expression softening. "I know you want to protect us, Silas. But sometimes the best way to fight is to hold your ground. We can't let them dictate our actions. Not now, when we're so close to understanding what we're up against."

Silas nodded, his jaw tightening as he forced himself to focus. The shadows continued to taunt them, their movements erratic and menacing, but he refused to give them the satisfaction of a reaction. Instead, he turned back to the table, his gaze falling once more on the ancient text.

Helena joined him, her fingers flipping carefully through the pages as she searched for anything they might have overlooked. The illustrations were haunting—twisting, amorphous shapes that seemed to blur and shift even on the page, accompanied by descriptions of creatures that existed beyond the boundaries of light and shadow.

"It says here that these... beings," Helena began, her voice hesitant, "are bound to the old ones' will. They exist in a liminal state, somewhere between the physical and the ethereal, which is why they can move the way they do. They're drawn to power, particularly to sources of light."

"Like Isabelle," Silas said grimly, the pieces falling into place.

Helena nodded. "Exactly. Her light is a threat to them, but it also attracts them. The stronger her power grows, the more they'll come for her."

Silas's chest tightened, his thoughts once again turning dark. Isabelle was the center of everything, his world, his heart, and now, the key to a battle that stretched beyond anything he could fully comprehend. The idea of losing her, of failing to protect her from forces he couldn't see or understand, was almost too much to bear.

"We have to find a way to shield her," Silas said, his voice firm. "There has to be something in this book, some way to protect her light without suppressing it."

Helena flipped another page, her gaze scanning the dense text. "There might be," she said softly. "But we need time to piece it together. The rituals described here... they're complex. Ancient. And if we get it wrong..." She didn't finish the thought, but the weight of her words hung heavy in the air.

Silas nodded, his resolve hardening. "Then we don't get it wrong. We figure this out. We keep her safe, no matter what it takes."

The shadows outside seemed to grow restless, their movements more frantic, as though sensing their failure to provoke Silas into action. He cast a wary glance at the window, his jaw tightening as he ignored their taunts.

Helena placed a hand on his arm, her gaze steady. "We'll get through this, Silas. Together. But we can't let them distract us. Focus on the book. Focus on Isabelle."

Silas looked at her, the gratitude clear in his eyes. "Thank you, Helena," he said quietly. "For everything."

She offered a faint smile, though the worry in her eyes didn't fade. "We're in this together. All of us."

As they returned to the table, the shadows outside began to fade, their presence receding as though they had realized their efforts were futile. But Silas knew they would return. They always did.

And as he and Helena continued to delve into the ancient text, Silas's mind remained sharp, his resolve unshaken. Whatever the shadows had planned, whatever dangers lay ahead, he would face them. For Isabelle, for their future, and for the light that had brought him out of his own darkness.

Chapter Twenty-Four

The Veil of Memories

The mansion was cloaked in stillness, its grand halls dimly lit by the flickering light of a single lamp in the drawing room. Helena had retired to her quarters after hours of pouring over The Chronicles of the Forgotten Ones, her exhaustion palpable as she excused herself, leaving Silas alone with his thoughts. The heavy tome lay open on the table before him, its ancient pages filled with cryptic texts and haunting illustrations.

Silas sat motionless, his gaze fixed on the words, though his mind drifted elsewhere. The shadows outside had faded, but their lingering presence had left an unease that refused to dissipate. He leaned back in his chair, his fingers brushing absently over the edge of the book as memories from long ago began to resurface, unbidden and vivid.

Ronan's voice echoed in his mind: "When the time is right, you will remember."

At first, the words had seemed cryptic, yet Silas now found himself grasping at them, searching for meaning. He closed his eyes, the weight of the night pressing down on him as fragments of his past rose to the surface......a memory he had long buried but could not ignore.

It had been centuries ago, a fleeting moment during a time when he had wandered the bustling streets of a city whose name he could no longer recall. He had been following a trail of whispers, rumors of something ancient and dark stirring among the people. The air had been thick with tension, and Silas had felt an instinctive unease, the sensation of being watched, of unseen eyes tracking his every move.

Among the crowds, a figure had stood out not for any distinct feature, but for the sheer sense of wrongness that clung to them. They had moved with the flow of people, their face obscured, their presence fleeting, yet Silas had felt their gaze like a knife at his back. He had tried to follow, but the figure had vanished as suddenly as they had appeared, leaving him with only the sense that something wasn't right.

And now, centuries later, the memory felt sharper, more significant. Had that figure been one of the old ones? A harbinger of their return? Or something else entirely?

Silas's chest tightened as he recalled the sensation of that moment the suffocating weight of the air, the way his instincts had screamed at him to remain cautious, to keep moving. Is this what Ronan was trying to tell me? he wondered. Was he warning me about them, about something I saw but didn't understand at the time?

The thought unsettled him, filling him with a mixture of frustration and dread. Ronan's cryptic nature had always been a source of tension between them, and now Silas found himself questioning whether his friend had withheld more than he realized.

The hours dragged on, the quiet of the mansion broken only by the occasional creak of the walls or the distant sound of the wind outside. Silas remained seated, his eyes scanning the pages of the book with a determined focus. Helena's absence left him feeling more alone than usual, though he knew she needed rest. She had done more than her share tonight, unearthing truths that had brought them closer to understanding the danger they faced.

As he read, Silas's gaze fell on a passage near the back of the book, written in a script that was denser and more ornate than the rest. The words seemed to blur slightly, as though the very act of reading them required more effort, but Silas pressed on, his curiosity overriding his exhaustion.

The passage spoke of a place, a location that seemed to hold significance to the old ones: The Shrouded Vale.

The description was sparse, yet it was enough to stir something in Silas's memory. The Shrouded Vale was said to be a place hidden from mortal sight, cloaked in perpetual mist, where time itself bent and twisted. The text described it as a sanctuary for ancient powers, a place where the veil between worlds was thinnest, allowing the old ones to exert their influence even in slumber.

Silas felt a chill run through him as he absorbed the implications. If the old ones had a sanctuary, a place of power where they could gather strength, then it was likely the key to understanding their plans and possibly stopping them. But the text also carried a warning: "To seek the Vale is to seek the heart of the storm. Only those bound by the ancient threads may pass unharmed."

The words filled Silas with unease. Bound by the ancient threads. Did that mean the Shere bloodline? His bloodline? And if so, was it fate or a curse that tied him to this unfolding battle?

His thoughts darkened, his emotions swirling as he considered the weight of his lineage, the legacy he had only recently begun to understand. He had spent centuries cursing his existence, his vampiric nature, but now he found himself questioning whether his entire life had been leading to this moment, to this fight.

What if I was always meant to confront the old ones? he thought bitterly. What if everything every loss, every pain was building to this?

The candle burned low as the night wore on, and Silas stood, unable to remain seated any longer. He moved to the window, staring out into the darkness, his keen eyes searching the shadows for any sign of movement. The memory of that figure from his past lingered in his mind, a reminder that the old ones had always been closer than he realized.

His hand rested against the glass, his reflection faint in the dim light. "What are you trying to tell me, Ronan?" he muttered under his breath, his voice filled with frustration. "What is it I'm supposed to remember?"

Behind him, the open book seemed to hum with a quiet energy, its presence a constant reminder of the truths it contained. Silas turned, his gaze falling on the tome as though it might provide answers to the questions that gnawed at him.

But even as he returned to his seat, his mind remained restless. The mention of the Shrouded Vale had sparked something in him, a determination that burned brighter with each passing moment. If the old ones were hiding there, if their sanctuary truly existed, then he had to find it. He had to uncover its secrets, no matter the cost.

As dawn began to break, casting a faint glow over the horizon, Silas sat in the stillness of the drawing room, the book open before him, his mind filled with the weight of what lay ahead. Helena's words from earlier that night echoed in his mind, a reminder of the trust and loyalty they shared.

You're not alone in this.

For now, it was enough to steady him, to keep him focused. The road to the Shrouded Vale would be treacherous, but Silas knew he had no choice. The old ones were stirring, their presence growing stronger with each passing day, and if he didn't act, they would consume every-thing he held dear.

And as he prepared himself for the battles ahead, he made a silent vow: I will protect Isabelle. I will protect Helena. And I will uncover the truth of the Vale, even if it destroys me.

The mansion remained cloaked in silence as the candle burned low beside Silas. He had not slept. His mind, heavy with the weight of ancient secrets and unsettling visions, refused to rest. Though The Chronicles of the Forgotten Ones remained open before him, its inked symbols seeming to pulse with silent warning, he found no peace in its words not now, not yet.

His thoughts, thick with dread and questions, clawed at him. The Shrouded Vale. The faceless figure in the crowd from a century long gone. Ronan's cryptic words whispering through his memory like drifting fog: "When the time is right, you will remember."

With a quiet exhale, Silas leaned back and reached to the side table where a familiar book of poems rested beneath his half-empty cup of cold coffee. It was a simple thing, an old, slim volume with a cracked spine and dog-eared pages. Mark Gordon's Still as the Dust Settles. A collection of verses Silas had turned to again and again over the years when the centuries bore down too heavily, when the endless nights and the darkness within threatened to unravel him.

He thumbed through the pages with care, his hands gentler with this book than with most things. The smell of the old paper, faintly earthy and tinged with coffee stains, was oddly grounding.

And there it was.

His favourite, 'The Soothing Words'

He whispered the words aloud, as if reciting them might keep the gathering shadows at bay:

In secret, he wishes to breathe

butterfly kisses across her neck

but the moon and unseen forces

dedicate his thirst

to something else. From where

does this lust arise? He asks the moon

but only gets back a pocketful

of wavering light for an answer.

He will ask her again for that walk

in the meadow, forget the fear

of where it might end,

pretend for an hour

that he is as vulnerable as she

failing skin, always a heartbeat

from death, not condemned like him

to prowl forever.

Silas closed the book gently and held it to his chest.

The ache that lived beneath his ribs, a sorrow he rarely allowed himself to feel fully, rose with quiet grace. The poem was a mirror, painful in its reflection. It captured everything he was too afraid to say aloud, the yearning to be close to Isabelle without fear, without his monstrous thirst hanging over them; the ache to simply exist with her in the sunlit meadow of a dream, fragile and mortal, even for just an hour.

Not condemned. Not eternal. Just... together.

He felt a strange calm spread through him, fragile but soothing, like the last light of dusk before night claims the sky. These words were a balm to the fury twisting inside him, softening the sharp edges of his frustration and helplessness.

He sat there in the soft stillness, the ancient book of prophecies on one side, and the book of poems pressed to his heart.

One filled with warnings of doom.

The other, with reminders of why he still fought.

The shadows beyond the mansion may still lurk, waiting for their chance. The path to the Shrouded Vale may yet demand everything of him. But for this moment, Silas allowed himself peace.

And in the quiet, he whispered to the ghost of his memory, to the figure in the mist and the voice that echoed in his mind, "I remember now. I see the pieces... and I will find the whole."

CHAPTER TWENTY-FIVE

THE LIGHT BETWEEN SHADOWS

Morning in the mansion did not bring sunlight.

Only a pale grey twilight filtered in through the towering windows, muted by the storm-bloated clouds that pressed heavily against the sky. The wind outside whispered like a forgotten lullaby, caressing the old stone walls, and carrying with it the faint scent of rain, moss, and distant memory.

Inside, the drawing room still bore the hush of night. The candle Silas had burned through the long hours had long since died, leaving only the soft glow of a low-burning fireplace in its place. The embers crackled with a slow, rhythmic sigh, casting long shadows that danced across the ornate bookshelves and velvet drapes like spectres waiting to be named.

Silas had not moved from the high-backed chair by the hearth. His body was still, carved in quiet contemplation, the worn book of poetry still resting in his lap. His gaze was fixed not on the flames but somewhere beyond them somewhere lost in memory and meaning.

A profound stillness had settled over him, like the air before a storm. But within that silence, his heart roared with emotion.

Last night's discoveries had shifted something inside him, The Chronicles of the Forgotten Ones, the revelation of the Shrouded Vale, the memory of the figure from the crowd whose face he had never seen but whose presence had whispered of ancient blood and buried truths. The ache that had lingered for centuries within his undead heart now pulsed with a deeper, more present weight.

He exhaled slowly, rubbing a hand over his face, the faint scrape of stubble against his palm grounding him. His thoughts spiralled, but they always came back to one name.

Isabelle.

Her light had become the axis around which his world turned. And yet... her light also cast shadows he could not yet define. Was she the key to salvation or sacrifice?

The poem, he thought, glancing at the open page resting on his lap. It lingered in his mind like a prayer, its final lines wrapping around him like a lover's embrace:

"Failing skin, always a heartbeat from death, not condemned like him to prowl forever."

Silas blinked hard, his jaw tightening.

How many lifetimes had he watched humanity slip through his fingers? How many women had he touched with trembling hands only to feel them grow cold within decades, while he remained unchanged? Isabelle was different—is different. And yet now, with her awakening as a Celestial, he wondered if her destiny would be ripped from his hands once more, not by age, but by power.

A gentle creak broke the silence. Silas looked up.

Helena stood in the archway of the drawing room, a robe drawn tight around her slender frame, her hair mussed from sleep. She looked tired, but alert, her gaze instantly falling to the ancient book still open on the table beside Silas.

"You didn't sleep," she said softly, stepping into the room.

"No." His voice was raw, but steady.

She crossed to the window and pulled back the heavy curtain slightly, peering out at the shifting fog beyond. "The shadows haven't returned. At least... not in the same way."

Silas didn't answer. His mind remained fixed on the Vale, on the passage he had read over and over through the night, the words etched into him now like runes on stone.

"Only those bound by the ancient threads may pass unharmed."

What threads bound him? What thread bound Isabelle? Was it love? Fate? Or something far older?

"You look like a man who's on the edge of a cliff," Helena murmured, her voice breaking gently into his thoughts.

He looked up at her, eyes hollow and searching. "What if I've already fallen?"

She moved closer, placing a hand on his shoulder. "You haven't. You're still here. Still fighting. That matters."

Silas exhaled, resting his head briefly against her hand before pulling back. "The Shrouded Vale," he said. "I believe it's real. The book confirms what Ronan hinted at. I saw it once in a vision, or maybe just a dream. A place wrapped in fog and silence, the air like silk and ash. I was drawn to it then... and I'm being drawn to it now."

Helena's eyes narrowed. "And you believe the old ones are there?"

"I believe they sleep there," Silas said. "Or something close to sleep. The book speaks of a 'thin place,' a world between breath and oblivion where time forgets itself. The Vale. I think it's where they go to gather strength. It might also be the only place we can stop them before they awaken fully."

Helena's lips parted; her voice hesitant. "And what about Isabelle?"

Silas's throat constricted.

He turned away, walking to the window. The fog outside twisted slowly through the trees like fingers searching for a soul. "She doesn't know what's coming," he said. "And I don't know how much of her light I can protect her from how much of it she can survive."

Helena watched him in silence, her brow furrowed with empathy and a tension of her own.

"She loves you, Silas. That's not something ancient or dark. That's real. That's now."

He nodded, though his expression didn't change. "And I love her. Which is why I can't let my love cloud what must be done. If this Vale holds answers... then I have to go, there. Alone."

Helena's eyes widened. "Silas, no—"

He held up a hand, gently but firmly. "It's not a place for her. Not yet. Not until we know how to shield her from its pull." His eyes burned with resolve. "If I am bound by these ancient threads... then let me be the one to unravel them."

The fire in the hearth crackled, casting a glow that painted him in gold and shadow, as if the light itself were unsure of what he was becoming.

Helena was quiet for a long moment, then nodded slowly. "We'll help you prepare. You won't walk into this unarmed."

Silas finally allowed himself to sit again. The book of poems still lay open on his lap, and he placed a hand gently on it.

"This," he said, touching the verse, "reminds me of who I am. That I still feel. That I'm still capable of love." He looked at Helena. "But that book—" he nodded to The Chronicles "—that's who I might become. And I need to find out if I can be more than that."

The rain began to fall then, light and steady, against the window-panes like a song from some forgotten era.

The day had begun, but it brought no answers only the burden of choices, and the whisper of a place cloaked in mist where ancient evils stirred.

And Silas, eternal guardian, condemned lover, bound by threads unseen, would walk toward it.

Alone.

Chapter Twenty-Six

A Memory Unearthed

The rain had not stopped since dawn. It fell in soft sheets across the mansion's high-paned windows, whispering secrets against the glass like a persistent ghost. Inside, the atmosphere remained thick with unspoken thoughts and the lingering dread of what was to come.

Silas stood by the hearth, the flames dancing low behind him, his posture tense and unmoving. The echoes of Helena's words still lingered in the corners of the room, but his thoughts had drifted elsewhere somewhere older, deeper, buried in the folds of time.

There was a memory, hazy, elusive that had begun to pulse to the surface. It tugged at him like a half-formed whisper, fragile but persistent.

He closed his eyes.

And then, he saw it.

A book.

One he hadn't thought of in over a century.

It had been tucked away in a hidden corner of a forgotten library in Eastern Europe mildewed and brittle with age. He had read it in a single sitting beneath the cracked glass dome of an abandoned reading hall, intrigued by its strangeness, though at the time, it had felt more like madness than meaning. But some how it made it way to New York, by whom was unknow unless.... It was a message.

It had been called The Blood of the Hollowed, written in a dead dialect that only a few remaining scholars could comprehend. It had spoken in riddles, metaphors cloaked in symbols, talking of "vessels of twilight" and "the echo of the Vale," phrases that had made little sense back then. But now, with the Shrouded Vale clear in his mind and the pieces aligning like constellations, he realized—the book had been speaking of the old ones.

And perhaps how to stop them.

His eyes snapped open. "I have to find it," he said aloud, turning swiftly.

Helena looked up from where she sat studying The Chronicles of the Forgotten Ones, startled. "Find what?"

"A book," he said, already moving toward the door, his coat swinging over his shoulders. "One I read over a hundred years ago. It didn't make sense to me then. Now it might."

"Silas wait," Helena stood quickly, frowning. "It's dangerous to go out there alone, especially after last night. The shadows—"

"I know," he said sharply, then softened his voice. "But I have to. I'll move fast."

And with that, he was gone.

The city blurred beneath his feet. Silas moved with inhuman speed, his long coat snapping behind him as he raced through the rain-slicked streets, past blinking traffic lights and shuttered storefronts. His destination: the old library beneath the catacombs on the east side of the city what had once been a monastery, long since converted to a historical archive and then forgotten again.

But as he neared the vine-covered steps that descended into the underground alcove, he felt it.

A presence.

No several.

He skidded to a halt just outside the rusted gate, fangs baring instinctively as five forms emerged from the shadows lean, gaunt vampires with pale, almost translucent skin stretched over sinewy frames. Their eyes glowed a sickly silver, not the crimson of his kind, and their mouths were already parting with a hiss, fangs elongated, their bodies twitching like predators high on bloodlust.

Not normal. Not born like us.

Their scent was wrong. Old, but not aged. Feral.

He growled, readying himself. "You picked the wrong night."

They lunged in a blur of movement.

Silas dodged the first, sweeping a kick that shattered a ribcage, then spun to slam a stake through the chest of another but it barely staggered the creature. These weren't regular vampires. They didn't scream or turn to ash. They breathed, rattled like something kept alive by unnatural means.

One clamped onto his shoulder, and another raked claws down his side. Silas roared and twisted, driving his elbow into a skull hard enough to break it, but the vampire only shrieked with laughter, blood dripping from its mouth.

He was outnumbered.

And he was bleeding.

For the first time in centuries, he felt the pain not receding.

He wasn't healing.

Panic flared for half a second. What the hell are these things?

And then, A blur, A blade, A familiar snarl.

Ronan.

He erupted from the rain like vengeance given form, slicing through the vampires with a black-bladed sword humming with ancient runes. One creature fell instantly, its head rolling across the pavement in a hiss of steam. Another leapt at him, but Ronan spun, impaling it mid-air and pinning it to the crumbling library wall.

"They're hybrids," Ronan said through gritted teeth. "Spliced from old blood. Experiments. I've seen whispers of them, but never this close to the surface."

Silas slumped slightly, gritting his teeth as he staggered back to his feet. "They're not dying like they should."

"Because they were never meant to," Ronan spat, hacking through the last creature's chest. "They were created to last."

The final vampire let out a wet, gurgling screech before falling still, twitching in the muck. The street fell silent except for the soft hiss of rain and Silas's ragged breath.

He clutched his side, the wound burned and still... no healing.

"Come on," Ronan said, slipping an arm under Silas's to steady him. "Let's get you back. You're in no condition to fight."

Back at the mansion, Helena rushed to meet them as they entered, her eyes wide with panic at the sight of Silas's blood.

"Put him down on the table, quickly."

She didn't wait. Her hands were already working, reaching for pouches of herbs and salves from the apothecary drawers she kept near the hearth. The scent of crushed sage, lavender, and vervain filled the air as she poured hot water over a tincture of green leaves and began applying the salve to Silas's wound.

He groaned at the contact.

"It burns," he hissed.

"It's meant to," Helena replied with gentle firmness. "These herbs were used by witches long ago to fight corrupted blood. You're lucky it didn't spread further."

Ronan stood nearby, watching silently as Helena worked. "They weren't like us," he said. "They moved differently. Fought like soldiers. But they weren't born. They were made."

"Who would make such things?" Helena asked, tying a poultice tightly around Silas's ribs.

Silas answered, his voice strained but sure.

"The old ones."

A tense silence followed.

Then he turned to Helena. "I need that book. The Blood of the Hollowed. It's in that library. I saw it. We need it before they burn it or bury it again."

Helena nodded. "We'll go. But not tonight. You're not going any-where for a few hours."

Silas exhaled, his head falling back against the table, his breath slow and ragged.

As the fire crackled again to life, the rain softened, but the mansion now felt different.

As if something had shifted in the world outside.

They weren't just being watched anymore.

They were being hunted.

Chapter Twenty-Seven

Bonds Forged in Fire

The day had surrendered to a sullen dusk. Rain no longer fell, but the ground was soaked in its memory, and low clouds stretched like bruises across the sky. Fog curled like smoke along the mansion's outer gardens, rising from the wet stone paths and hedgerows, as if the earth itself exhaled unease. The world outside held its breath—too still, too watchful.

Inside, the drawing room was cloaked in warm amber light. The tall hearth crackled softly, casting a gentle glow that flickered over the bookshelves and polished wood panels. Shadows swayed across the walls like slow dancers, not sinister, but heavy with knowing. A thin wisp of incense hung in the air—clove, sandalwood, and something faintly metallic—burning from a small copper dish Helena had lit earlier to clear the energy after the hybrids' attack.

Silas stood before the fire, his form backlit by the glow, still partially bandaged beneath his black shirt. Despite the stiffness in his shoulders, there was something almost noble in the sway he stood like a warrior returned from war, weathered but not broken. Helena was seated beside the hearth, the book The Blood of the Hollowed open across her knees. Isabelle remained by the window, staring out into the mist-shrouded gardens with a faraway look, the light from the fire catching in her eyes like starlight trapped in glass.

The silence was a living thing.

Then the doors creaked open with slow ceremony.

The tension in the room coiled tighter as a tall figure emerged from the corridor.

Ronan.

He stepped into the warmth with a hunter's grace, the rain still clinging to his coat like dew on black silk. His presence was quiet, but it filled the room like thunder in the distance felt before it was heard.

The flicker of light caught the edge of his blade where it rested sheathed at his back, and the moment he entered, the fire seemed to dim for the briefest instant, as though acknowledging something older, deeper. Not darker but undeniably powerful.

His gaze moved to each of them in turn.

To Helena, measuring, respectful.

To Silas, familiar, knowing.

And then... to Isabelle.

That was when the stillness broke.

He stopped.

There was something unspoken in the air, like the shift of gravity.

Ronan's eyes softened, just slightly, their edge melting into something almost reverent. His senses confirmed what he had already suspected: Isabelle's aura burned brighter than any being he'd encountered in centuries. But it wasn't just power it was purity. A flame that hadn't been corrupted by time, blood, or darkness.

"Celestial..." he murmured, almost under his breath. "So, it's true."

Isabelle tilted her head, cautious but curious. "You know what I am?"

Ronan didn't answer immediately. Instead, he gave a slight bow, something oddly formal. "I suspected. Now I know. The light... it sings around you, like it remembers a melody long lost."

She looked to Silas for reassurance, and he gave a gentle nod. "Ronan is an old friend. Trusted. He's been fighting longer than most of us have lived. He won't hurt you."

Ronan stepped closer, slowly, his expression shifting from awe to something more resolute. "I won't let anyone hurt you," he said firmly. "Whatever else happens... protecting you is now part of my purpose."

Helena, who had been observing silently, arched a brow at the sudden conviction in Ronan's tone. She sensed his words weren't just spoken from obligation but from instinct, something deeper, older, like a vow stitched into the fabric of his very soul.

"Ronan," Silas said after a long silence, "tell them what you told me... about the hybrids."

Ronan's jaw tightened as he folded his arms, leaning against the mantle. "They were once human," he said. "Taken from the fringes of society, outcasts, the dying, the broken. Manipulated, twisted by blood rituals derived from the old ones' teachings. Someone... or something... has begun resurrecting the process."

Helena swallowed, her brows knitting together. "And how many do you think there are?"

"At least a dozen we can be sure of," Ronan said grimly. "But if what I've seen is true, there could be entire clusters across cities. They hunt in silence. Avoid the old vampire haunts. They're building a new order one that doesn't follow vampire law, one that doesn't care for legacy or discretion. They serve only the hunger."

He looked directly at Silas. "You certainly know how to attract the hive."

Silas gave a humorless smile. "What can I say? They have a taste for trouble."

But his expression darkened quickly as the weight of it all settled in again.

"What about the book?" Helena asked, gesturing toward The Blood of the Hollowed, now resting atop the nearby desk.

Ronan turned toward it slowly, the corners of his mouth quirking upward in a faint, almost guilty smile. "That... was me."

Silas blinked. "You?"

"I took it from the ruins in Eastern Europe before anyone else could. It didn't belong there not anymore. It spoke of the Vale, of the old ones. I knew it would mean something to you someday... and to her." He nodded toward Isabelle. "So, I brought it to New York and left it in the city's deep archives. A quiet place, undisturbed by most of our kind. I even... planted the memory in your mind."

"You what?" Silas's voice was stunned, not angry, just incredulous.

"I couldn't know for sure when the time would come," Ronan replied calmly. "But I had to make sure you'd find it when it did. So, I left an echo. A thread in your mind. Subtle, fragile, but enough that it would stir when it was needed."

Silas stared at him for a long moment. "You always were a step ahead."

"I had time," Ronan said dryly. "A few centuries of hiding in the shadows will do that."

Helena moved toward the desk, fingers skimming the edge of the book's cracked leather spine. "You said it contains more than riddles now that we understand the context. What exactly are we looking for in this?"

Ronan's expression sobered. "Clues. References. The Vale is more than a place it's a convergence. A point of weakness in the fabric between realms. If the old ones wake there, they'll step into our world stronger than ever before. This book doesn't tell us how to defeat them... but it tells us where they bleed."

"Where they bleed..." Helena echoed, unsettled.

"They're not gods," Ronan said. "They just think they are. And somewhere in that text, I believe, is the map to their mortality."

Isabelle, quiet until now, took a step forward. "And what happens if I'm not strong enough?"

Ronan turned to her; his voice softer now. "You will be. You were made for this. You are light in its rarest form, Isabelle. But light cannot stand alone. It needs shadow to give it shape. Silas is your anchor. Helena your guide. And I..." He paused, a small wry smile ghosting his lips. "I suppose I'm your sword."

Silas met his eyes and nodded once silent gratitude, silent trust.

Outside, the rain had ceased.

But in the wind that swept through the cracked chimney flues, they could all hear it:

Something was coming.

And it would not come quietly.

The tension in the drawing room had eased slightly, but only just. Ronan now stood by the long oak table where The Blood of the Hollowed lay open, fingers brushing its fragile edge with the reverence of one handling a sacred relic.

The fire hissed and popped quietly in the hearth behind them, and the flames' reflection danced over Ronan's face, illuminating the haunted edges of his expression. For all his power and certainty, there was a heaviness behind his eyes like someone who had already buried too many truths and feared unearthing more.

Silas leaned against the mantle, arms crossed tightly over his chest, his gaze flickering between Ronan and the book. He could feel the weight of the room - the weight of what was coming—pressing down on his chest like iron. He had always trusted Ronan, but there was something unspoken in the air, something his friend wasn't yet saying.

"You knew what she was," Silas said at last, his voice low.

Ronan's jaw flexed, eyes narrowing slightly not in anger, but in restraint. "I suspected," he admitted. "I've seen only one other Celestial in my life, and even then, only briefly. Isabelle's light is different. Stronger. It resonates. Like something ancient finally remembered its own name."

He turned then to face her fully, his voice gentling. "It's not just that you're rare, Isabelle. It's that you were born now. In this time. When the world is tipping."

Across the room, Isabelle stood near the tall windows, her arms crossed over her chest, gaze still distant. But at Ronan's words, her expression cracked slightly, her jaw tightening as her fingers gripped the fabric of her sleeve.

She spoke without looking at him. "You say that like I chose this."

Ronan's voice softened. "You didn't. Destiny never asks permission."

That struck her deeply.

Her eyes finally met his, and what shimmered there wasn't power it was fear.

"I don't know how to be what you think I am," she whispered. "I feel it, yes something inside me waking but I don't understand it. And every time it stirs, it feels like something else is being pushed away. Like I'm losing myself."

Silas stepped toward her, instinct pulling him close. He gently touched her hand. "You're still you, Isabelle. Nothing can change that. Not even light that burns like the stars."

She nodded once, barely, but her thoughts remained tangled.

I'm not just changing, she thought. I'm becoming something I don't understand... and everyone else seems to believe I already am.

The pressure, the quiet expectation was overwhelming. She wanted to be strong for Silas, for Helena, for this cause she barely comprehended. But inside her chest, the unknown throbbed like a second heartbeat, unfamiliar and wild.

Helena watched them from the far side of the room, her heart aching quietly. She had never felt more protective of Isabelle than she did now. The young woman's bravery stirred something maternal in her a need to shelter her from the darkness growing just beyond their reach.

But Helena's gaze eventually shifted to Silas, her eyes narrowing slightly.

He hadn't said it yet, but she knew.

He was going to face the old ones alone.

Her thoughts turned inward, heavy and conflicted.

He's always borne too much on his shoulders, she thought. Too willing to sacrifice, too quick to step into the fire. But this time... this time it may cost him everything.

She rose to her feet, voice firm yet tender. "Silas, if you're thinking of going into the Vale alone—"

"I have to," he interrupted softly, but with finality.

Helena stepped closer, eyes flashing. "You think you're protecting us. But this isn't a war you can win alone. Even if you find them, what then? You'll fight them with what? Will? Rage?"

Ronan broke the tension with a grim nod. "She's right. You're strong, Silas but even I wouldn't walk into the Vale without knowing what I'd find. That place is older than time. It bends reality."

Silas looked down for a moment, then met Helena's gaze. "It has to be me. I'm tied to them. You saw the text. I'm 'bound by the ancient threads.' My blood... something in me is connected to the old ones. And if that's true, then maybe I'm the only one who can get close enough to learn how to stop them."

The room fell silent again.

The fire's light danced higher for a moment, as if answering the gravity of his words.

Chapter Twenty-Eight

The Storm Beneath

Outside, the wind had picked up again, rattling the windows in sharp bursts like impatient fingers. A storm was building far off, but inevitable.

Inside, the world held its breath.

Ronan remained by the book, eyes lowered, fingers now tracing a passage in the margin of one of the final pages. His voice, when it came, was thoughtful.

"You said you remembered this book, Silas. That something pulled it from memory."

Silas nodded slowly.

Ronan gave a faint smile. "That was me. I put the image there. I didn't know when you'd remember. But I trusted you would when the time was right."

Silas exhaled, the memory flickering behind his eyes dim light, dust-choked air, a strange page that had made no sense to a younger, more reckless version of himself. He'd thought it nonsense.

Now he knew better.

Helena crossed to Ronan's side, peering over his shoulder at the page. "What does this part mean?" she asked, pointing to a passage inscribed in crimson ink, its letters warped and looping like thorned vines.

Ronan's expression darkened. "It says: 'When the breath of twilight folds, and the stars turn their backs, the door will open not with blood but with betrayal.'"

Helena looked up; brow furrowed. "Betrayal?"

Isabelle's voice, soft but certain, broke the tension. "It means someone close to us... may already be marked."

The words chilled the room.

Ronan said nothing, but his hand clenched into a fist.

Silas stared into the fire.

His mind was spinning. He felt the pieces shifting, aligning just out of reach. The Vale, the hybrids, Isabelle's awakening, and now... betrayal.

It wasn't just a fight for survival anymore.

It was a reckoning.

And it was already underway.

Chapter Twenty-Nine

The Veil Trembles

The air in the mansion had changed.

It was no longer still it shivered.

A low hum vibrated beneath the silence, as if the house itself sensed what was to come. Shadows clung tighter to the corners, stretching longer even in the warm firelight. Every flicker of candle flame felt like a heartbeat pulsing in tandem with the growing storm outside.

Silas stood in the war room, which until now had never been needed for actual war.

The long oak table was strewn with maps, books, faded glyphs on scrolls written in languages lost before empires were born. The great chandelier above cast a muted gold light over it all, but nothing about the scene felt comforting.

Helena was carefully packing satchels with tinctures, herbs, and protective totems. She moved methodically, but there was a tension in her shoulders, as if every second closer to departure wound her tighter.

Ronan stood by the tall window, watching the fog deepen beyond the iron gates. He hadn't spoken in the last ten minutes, but Silas knew what he was thinking. The Vale was calling.

And Isabelle...

She stood apart, near the fireplace, her arms crossed, her lips pressed into a line of thoughtful dread. Her usual warmth felt dimmed still present but buried under a weight she hadn't chosen and didn't know how to lift.

Silas's Thoughts

Silas looked at each of them and felt the burden settle heavier across his chest. He had asked them to walk into the mouth of a storm. And they hadn't hesitated.

Even Ronan.

Even Isabelle.

But still, doubt gnawed at him.

How do I protect the woman I love from a fate neither of us understand?

How do I confront the ancient thing I may be tied to... and still return human enough to be hers?

The thought of losing her no, of her losing herself was unbearable.

He moved toward her now, quietly.

Isabelle looked up as he approached, her eyes reflecting the firelight like polished amber. "You're afraid," she said softly.

"I am," he admitted. "But not for myself."

She nodded, understanding. "I feel like I'm standing at the edge of something... and I don't know if it's a beginning or an end."

He reached out, brushing his fingers gently along her jaw. "No matter what we find in the Vale, Isabelle, I need you to know something."

She leaned into his touch.

"I'd walk into any darkness for you. I have. And I will again. But if it ever comes to choosing between that light inside of you... and me?" He hesitated, swallowing hard. "Choose the light. Always."

Her eyes shimmered with emotion, her voice barely a whisper. "What if the light chooses you?"

They kissed then slow, deliberate, filled with a longing that only lovers caught between worlds can know. The kind of kiss that wasn't meant for now, but for always.

Helena's Thoughts

Helena paused as she watched them from across the room, her heart a knot of emotions. She had seen so much over the centuries. War. Love. Loss. But never had she witnessed something like these two souls drawn by fate into a war older than time itself.

And now, she thought, he wants to go into the Vale alone.

Her fingers clenched around the pouch of grave-root powder.

Not if I can help it.

She would walk beside them through the storm if needed. She had read every line of the Chronicles, every hidden verse of The Blood of the Hollowed. The danger they faced was beyond death. And they would need more than blades and spells.

They would need one another.

Ronan's Thoughts

At the window, Ronan's sharp eyes scanned the shifting fog. It moved unnaturally now—not with the slow grace of mist but with the restless pulse of breath. Something watched from within it. Something old. Something eager.

He had felt it in the Vale. He felt it now.

They know.

They're stirring.

The old ones would not wait much longer.

And worse still something was coming to stop them from even beginning the journey.

The Disruption

A sharp crack split the air.

The chandeliers flickered wildly.

Then came the scream not from within the mansion but outside followed by the shrill wail of metal against stone.

Ronan turned instantly. "We're not alone."

Silas was already moving, grabbing the curved blade hidden beneath the map table. Isabelle's hand flared with light as she instinctively summoned the strange energy within her. It shimmered down her arm, crackling across her skin like divine fire barely contained.

Helena dropped her satchels, grabbing the hilt of a small blade coated in protective oils. "It's not just hybrids," she said, voice trembling. "Something else is with them."

They ran down the hall, the marble floors echoing with the urgency of boots and breath.

As they burst through the front doors, the storm wind hit them full force cold, thick with the scent of scorched soil and blood.

Figures moved at the edge of the garden the same pale hybrids they had fought before. But this time, they were not alone.

In the centre of the stone path stood a tall, hunched creature cloaked in layered, tattered robes. Its skin was grey as ash, and long black tendrils of hair swayed in the wind. No eyes, only deep hollow sockets that glowed faintly violet.

Silas froze.

"That's not a hybrid," Ronan said tightly. "That's something from the Vale."

The creature raised a skeletal hand, and the fog behind it pulsed warped as if the air itself bowed to its command.

And then it spoke.

A voice like falling stones.

"You cannot unmake what was written. The Vale calls its own."

It raised its hand, and the hybrids charged.

Chapter Thirty

When the Vale Opens

The moment froze in time.

The fog rolled across the garden like a living tide, sliding over the grass, between twisted hedges, curling around the wrought iron gates like serpents returning to a nest.

The creature at the centre the Vale Wraith, Helena would call it later stood perfectly still, robes tattered and weightless, its hollow eyes shimmering like dead stars. The wind didn't touch it. It existed beyond the weather, beyond breath.

Behind it, the hybrids lurched forward feral, twitching, eyes shining with silver hunger.

Silas felt every inch of his body tense, his vampiric senses igniting like wildfire. The pressure in the air was suffocating, like standing at the edge of a cliff and staring down into eternity. Yet in that single moment, with the storm around them and the enemy charging, his thoughts were only of her.

Isabelle.

He looked over.

She stood a few feet behind him, radiant and still, her face a canvas of dread and defiance. Light shimmered faintly around her fingers uncontrolled, instinctive. The energy was alive beneath her skin, burning with a power she had not yet claimed.

Fear gripped her heart like a fist. But it wasn't for herself.

It was for Silas.

She'd seen him bleed, and he hadn't healed. She'd felt the weight on his shoulders, the self-sacrificing resolve in his voice. He would face the Vale alone if they let him.

But she wouldn't.

She couldn't.

If fate had given her this light, then she would wield it not as a weapon... but as a promise.

The Charge

The first hybrid lunged, shrieking with inhuman rage.

Silas met it mid-air with a savage swing of his curved blade, sending it crashing into the stone path with a wet crunch. Two more followed, flanking him, clawed hands flashing.

Ronan was already beside him, his blade a blur of motion elegant and brutal. "They're faster this time," he growled, driving his sword through a hybrid's chest and twisting. "More refined. Less wild."

Helena stayed close to Isabelle, drawing sigils into the air with swift, practiced fingers. "Protective wards stay behind me!" she shouted, her voice edged with panic and precision.

But the Wraith was moving now.

It didn't run. It glided, smooth and soundless, its hands outstretched toward the mansion doors like it already owned the place like it belonged.

Silas locked eyes with it, the world narrowing around him.

"You were marked before you were born, child of blood and ash."

"The Vale remembers its heir."

The words pierced him like shards of ice. He staggered slightly.

Ronan cursed. "Silas, do not listen those things twist truth into chains!"

But it was too late.

The Wraith raised both hands, and with a force like a collapsing star, it sent out a concussive blast of violet energy. The ground cracked, statues shattered, and both Silas and Ronan were thrown back into the side garden wall.

Silas groaned, blood leaking from his mouth. He couldn't move. His bones were whole but wrong, like something inside was refusing to mend.

Isabelle's Awakening

Time slowed.

Isabelle saw Silas fall.

The man who had defied fate to protect her. The man who had given centuries of solitude for a single touch of her hand. The one who whispered promises not with words, but with the way he looked at her as if she was a miracle.

He was broken on the ground.

And in that moment, something in her snapped open.

Her scream split the fog like lightning.

The light within her erupted. It wasn't soft this time. It didn't flicker gently like it had before. It roared out of her in a wave of pure energy silver-gold and blinding, laced with fire and sorrow and fury.

The hybrids shrieked and melted, collapsing into ash before they could reach the door.

The Wraith turned sharply but too late.

Isabelle stepped forward, her entire body glowing like a fallen star. Her eyes burned with celestial light, and when she spoke, her voice was layered not just her own, but something older speaking through her.

"This is not your realm. You will not take him from me."

She lifted her hand.

The Wraith screeched, a horrid, echoing sound that cracked the night. The light struck it directly, bursting through its incorporeal form and sending it careening into the hedge wall, where it vanished into smoke and black flame.

Silence followed. Deafening, trembling silence.

Helena lowered her arms slowly, mouth slightly open.

Ronan stood, stunned, the sword limp in his hand.

Isabelle turned toward Silas, collapsing to her knees beside him. "Silas?" she whispered, brushing his bloodied cheek. "Please..."

His eyes fluttered.

He smiled weakly. "You... found it."

She blinked. "Found what?"

"The light... they spoke of. You..."

And then he passed out.

Aftermath

Back inside the mansion, the storm raged on outside, but within the walls there was only breath, firelight, and the ache of what had just passed.

Silas lay on the couch, Helena hovering over him, applying a fresh herbal poultice laced with celestial balm. His skin was raw where the energy had touched him, but already, faint signs of healing had returned—his body responding to her presence.

Ronan sat silently nearby, staring into the fire, his thoughts dark and deep. "That wasn't just an awakening," he muttered. "That was... inheritance."

Helena looked up. "What do you mean?"

He met her gaze. "Her power... it's old. Not just Celestial. Something woven into the fabric of the Vale itself. She didn't just repel that creature... she severed its tie to this plane."

Helena's breath caught. "You mean...?"

"She can banish them," Ronan said. "Not kill. Not wound. But erase their existence from this realm entirely."

They looked over at Isabelle, who sat at Silas's side, gently stroking his hair, her eyes unfocused, wide with the weight of what she'd done.

"I didn't mean to..." she whispered. "I didn't know I could."

Silas stirred beside her, groaning softly.

She bent closer. "I'm here," she whispered. "Always."

And for now, that was enough.

But in the deepest parts of the mansion, the old books trembled on their shelves.

And somewhere, in the hidden corners of the Shrouded Vale, something older than even the old ones... had begun to stir.

Chapter Thirty-One

The Stillness Before the Storm

The fire crackled quietly in the hearth, throwing long, languid shadows across the walls of the great hall. The mansion was silent, but it was not peace. It was aftermath the kind that comes before the realization that everything has changed, and nothing can return to what it was.

Isabelle sat beside Silas, her legs tucked under her, one hand still wrapped gently around his wrist. His breathing had stabilized. The bruised colour had begun to retreat from his skin, his body slowly knitting itself back together with a strength that was not entirely his own.

The light that had erupted from Isabelle had left a residue in the air—fine and shimmering, like golden dust, drifting lazily through the stillness. It clung to her skin, tangled in her lashes. But it was not the light that frightened her.

It was the emptiness left behind.

The moment she had unleashed that power, something deep inside her had torn open—and something even deeper had answered. And now that the glow had faded, Isabelle felt hollow, like a song half-remembered.

"I didn't know I could do that..." she whispered aloud, though no one had asked.

Helena, seated in a nearby armchair with her eyes dark with worry, replied gently, "Neither did they."

But Isabelle wasn't comforted. Her hands trembled slightly, the echo of that impossible energy still humming in her bones. The sensation of it—light that seared but didn't burn, that commanded but didn't ask permission—still haunted her.

She looked to Silas.

Her light had saved him. But what would it cost next time?

In the Shadow of the Vale...

Far from the warmth of the hearth, the Shrouded Vale was breathing.

The mists shifted, curling like smoke around blackened monoliths buried in the earth. Old trees stood dead and upright like rotting sentinels, their roots feeding on blood-soaked soil. And deep beneath the fractured land, something was waking.

The Wraith that Isabelle had banished did not return to its masters.

And the old ones had noticed.

From the deepest fissures in the stone came whispers languages that predated sound hissing in ancient cadence. The hybrids trembled in their hollows, their mutated forms writhing under invisible pressure. Something was stirring beneath the Vale that had not stirred in thousands of years.

The First Hunger.

The origin. The one from whom all darkness flowed.

They had not expected the girl.

They had not expected light.

Back at the Mansion...

Ronan stood at the window again, his arms crossed tightly, gaze locked on the distant storm still curling over the city's skyline like a creeping bruise.

He'd cleaned the blood from his blade, but not from his coat. The fight had been won—but not ended.

"We got lucky," he muttered, more to himself than anyone else.

Helena glanced up. "You think it will return?"

Ronan turned, his expression carved in shadow. "No. It won't. But something worse will."

Silas stirred then, groaning softly as he shifted upright on the couch. Isabelle was immediately at his side.

He smiled weakly. "Still here."

"You scared me," she whispered, and brushed her lips against his temple. "But I'm not letting you go anywhere now. Not again."

Silas leaned into her touch. "Not going far. But I can't stay behind."

He turned slowly to Ronan, whose jaw was tight with unspoken tension.

"You saw it too, didn't you?" Silas asked.

Ronan nodded. "The Vale is reacting. That was only the beginning. There's something... beneath it. Something older. That Wraith wasn't sent to kill you. It was testing boundaries. It wanted to know how far she could reach." He nodded toward Isabelle. "And now it knows."

Silas rose, still sore, but the fire in his eyes was returning.

Ronan watched him and smirked. "Just like old times, my friend."

Silas stretched, rotating his shoulder with a groan. "You can say that again."

They exchanged a look one forged in war, tempered in loss. The unspoken oath passed between them. Whatever came next, they would face it side by side.

The Call to Prepare

Helena stood now, brushing off her skirt. "We need to gather everything. If we go to the Vale, we'll need more than steel and instinct."

"I know what we'll need," Ronan said. He reached into the folds of his coat and pulled out a small leather pouch. From it, he drew a blood-coloured shard glowing faintly, like a pulse.

"A piece of the Threshold Stone," he explained. "One of the only things that can open the true gate to the Vale and let mortals through without breaking their minds. It will guide us. But once we enter... we can't come back the same."

Silas took the shard, his fingers brushing the pulsing edge.

Isabelle stepped forward. "I'm coming."

"No," Silas said instinctively. "Not until—"

"You don't get to decide that." she said softly but firmly. "Whatever this thing inside me is... it chose me. And I choose you. I'm not standing on the sidelines while you fight something that wants me as its prize."

Silas hesitated but the truth was, she had already proven stronger than all of them.

He nodded.

Ronan stepped forward, voice darker now. "Then we need to move quickly. I feel the veil thinning. The old ones will rise. And when they do..."

He looked between them, his family, his shield wall.

"...we fight the greatest war our kind has ever known."

Helena tightened the strap on her leather pouch, eyes hard.

Isabelle's hand found Silas's, her light already responding, wrapping around his fingers like a silent vow.

Silas looked out into the night and felt something stir in his bones do not fear, not even anger.

Purpose.

The time had come.

Chapter Thirty-Two

The Vision That Screamed

The fire had died to embers.

The air in the drawing room had thickened with exhaustion. Outside, the storm had ebbed, leaving the garden soaked and gleaming beneath a restless moon. Silas and Ronan sat at the long oak table, going over maps of ley lines, markers from The Blood of the Hollowed, and coordinates Helena had cross-referenced with half-burnt pages from the Chronicles.

Isabelle stood near the window, staring into the dark.

The fog was beginning to roll back into the trees. It moved slower now, like something watching, rather than reaching.

Her fingers trembled against the glass.

A chill began at the base of her spine. Not cold—not from the air. It was something internal. Like the breath had been drawn from her lungs and replaced with something old and unfamiliar.

She blinked.

And the world shifted.

The Vision

"Stop!"

The voice ripped through her head not her own, but within her. Her hands clutched at her temples as the room dissolved around her.

The mansion fell away in ribbons of smoke and gold.

She was somewhere else.

A meadow at first. Familiar. Bright.

She turned. Silas stood there, smiling at her beneath a sky that glowed lavender and rose. His eyes were kind, his hand reaching for hers.

She stepped toward him, then the sun vanished.

In its place, a black void tore through the clouds. The ground beneath her feet cracked, splitting into ash and fire. Silas's form twisted, his smile fading, replaced by a sharp, unnatural grin. His eyes went black. Wings of bone unfurled from his back, dripping with blood.

"No... no, no—"

His skin paled into stone, cracking and burning with violet fire. His voice deepened, ancient, inhuman.

"You made me this. Your light chose the wrong man."

She screamed.

Helena's voice called to her then, but from beneath her. She looked down and saw Helena crushed beneath a slab of stone, blood staining her once bright blouse. Her hand reached up toward Isabelle, trembling, fading.

"Isabelle, run..."

Then Ronan appeared, sword drawn, slashing wildly into an unseen horde of creatures, twisted, shrieking hybrids, and others... shadows that weren't shadows, burning with unholy flame. One of them pierced him through the chest. His mouth opened in a silent gasp. He looked at her—

Then fell.

"No! Please—stop!"

The sky screamed, the ground surged and then—

Back in the Mansion

Isabelle collapsed with a guttural cry, her knees hitting the floor hard. The crash silenced the room instantly.

Silas was the first to her side.

"Isabelle!"

Her breath came in ragged gasps. Her hands were shaking, her skin pale, lips parted as if trying to speak but the words were locked behind sheer, blinding terror.

Helena dropped to her knees beside her, hands on Isabelle's shoulders, grounding her. "It's a vision," she said quickly. "She's seen something."

Tears fell freely from Isabelle's eyes as she looked at them. "I saw—" she choked out, her voice cracked and raw, "I saw... you all die."

Helena's breath caught.

Silas froze, his entire body turning to ice.

"I saw you," Isabelle whispered, looking at Silas. "You changed. You... became one of them. You said I made you this way. Your eyes—your voice—Silas, it wasn't you." She clutched at his chest as if to anchor herself to his reality. "Helena was crushed. Ronan—Ronan died fighting them. I couldn't stop it—I couldn't stop any of it!"

Her body trembled with the memory, her voice breaking into sobs. "It felt real. Like I was there. Like I had already lost you."

Silas gathered her into his arms, holding her tightly as if he could somehow shield her from the dream's aftermath. His hand cradled the back of her head, his own heart pounding with a protective fury he couldn't express.

"That won't happen," he said firmly, fiercely. "I promise you. Not now. Not ever."

She shook her head against his chest. "But it felt like the truth."

Ronan stepped forward, calm but intense. "That's because they want it to feel real."

Helena looked up at him, still holding Isabelle's shaking hand. "What do you mean?"

Ronan's voice was quiet but edged with steel. "They're not just ancient. They're manipulative. They reach into the parts of you you're afraid to look at and they twist them. They show you futures that might be, not because they will happen, but because they want to weaken you before the battle begins."

He knelt beside Isabelle now, his grey eyes more human than she had ever seen them.

"They're trying to scare you. Trying to break you. And that vision? That was them altering your reality to stop you. To stop us."

Isabelle looked between them, her sobs easing slightly, though her body still trembled.

Silas wiped a tear from her cheek. "You're stronger than they think."

"You're stronger than they know," Helena added. "And we're still here. Together."

Isabelle took a breath. Shaky. But full.

The mansion around them felt warmer again, like the fire had found its pulse.

Silas leaned in close, his voice low. "We'll face whatever they send, Isabelle. But that vision? That isn't our fate. Not unless we let it be."

Her hand closed around his.

And this time, the light inside her did not burn—it held.

It glowed gently, like the steady flicker of a flame in the dark.

CHAPTER THIRTY-THREE

THE THRESHOLD BECKONS

The night was still when they departed.

It wasn't the silence of sleep or peace it was a breath held by the world itself. As though the earth, the sky, and every shadow in between understood that something was about to be unravelled. The moon hung low and pale, barely pushing light through the dense fog curling over the forest path.

The Threshold awaited.

They moved in silence beneath the canopy of skeletal trees, their footsteps muffled by moss and mist. Ronan led the way, the faint violet glow of the Threshold Stone pulsing steadily in his gloved hand.

The stone was unlike anything Isabelle had ever seen neither crystal nor gem, but something older. Shaped like a shard of a forgotten crown, jagged and slick like obsidian, it pulsed with a subtle heartbeat of light that seemed to breathe in unison with the surrounding darkness.

Helena walked beside Isabelle, her fingers tracing protective runes into the air as they moved, her lips silently murmuring old words not meant for modern ears. Her breath fogged in the cold, but her eyes remained sharp, unwavering.

Silas kept close to Isabelle, his body tense, senses sharpened. The image of her vision still haunted him, though he didn't show it. Every leaf rustle, every distant snap of twigs brought his hand closer to the hilt of his blade.

Ronan finally slowed as the trees thinned and the fog deepened into a wall of pale grey. The earth at their feet had changed no longer dirt or grass, but slate stone that shimmered faintly beneath their boots.

They had arrived.

The Threshold stood like a wound in the world a jagged rent of shifting light and shadow, barely discernible until you stood at its edge. It looked like the air itself had torn apart, and through that tear, something ancient, stared back.

Ronan turned to them, the Threshold Stone glowing steadily now in his palm.

"This is where the veil thins," he said. "Where the known world ends, and the Shrouded Vale begins."

The History of the Threshold Stone

Helena stepped closer, studying the stone with reverence.

"I've only read about it," she whispered. "They called it Alarion's Key. Said it was carved from the first tear shed by a dying god crystallized in the moment the realms separated. Only one is said to exist."

Ronan nodded. "It predates the old ones. Before them, there were gatekeepers—those who kept the balance between realms. When the gatekeepers fell, the Threshold Stone was lost for centuries."

Silas tilted his head. "Where did you find it?"

"Buried in the foundations of a sunken temple off the Croatian coast," Ronan said. "Guarded by something that didn't bleed when I struck it." His voice was cold, flat. "I didn't sleep for days after."

He handed the stone to Isabelle. The light in it flared briefly as it touched her skin.

"It recognizes her," Helena whispered.

"The stone responds to power tied to creation and entropy," Ronan confirmed. "To bloodlines like hers. And yours, Silas. The stone doesn't open a path...it binds you to the path."

Silas frowned. "Meaning?"

"Once we pass through... we're part of it. Seen. Tracked. The Vale remembers."

Crossing the Threshold

Isabelle stared into the shimmering veil. It hummed, not with sound, but with presence. As if a thousand voices were whispering beneath the surface, just out of hearing.

She turned to Silas, fear knotting her stomach.

"What if it changes us?"

He stepped closer, placing a steady hand on her cheek. "Then we change together."

She nodded, the light in her palm matching the pulse of the stone.

Ronan extended his hand toward the rippling wall of air and pressed the stone into it. The veil rippled violently then stilled.

A door formed made of fog and memory—and then slowly pulled open, revealing only darkness beyond.

Ronan stepped through first.

Then Helena.

Silas looked back once toward the life they were leaving behind.

And then he followed Isabelle through.

The Vale

Crossing the threshold was like falling without moving.

Cold swallowed them. The very air felt wrong thicker, older. It tasted of forgotten metal and ash. The sky was a perpetual dusk grey and violet, as if frozen in a storm that never quite broke.

They stood on a blackened plain cracked with glowing lines, like veins in dying stone. Strange trees arched overhead with leaves that whispered things when they fell. The light here didn't come from the sky, but from the ground soft and sickly, like the last breath of a candle.

Isabelle staggered slightly.

"I feel it," she murmured. "It knows we're here."

Silas took her hand.

"Then let it know we're ready."

Chapter Thirty-Four

What Was Buried, Now Awakens

The Vale greeted them with silence.

It was not the gentle kind that comforted, but the kind that pressed in thick and ancient. The air was weighty, as if each breath pulled centuries into their lungs. The light remained dim, fed not by sun or stars but by the veins of dull gold and violet that ran beneath the cracked obsidian earth. Every step they took stirred a low hum from the ground, as if the land itself was aware, and displeased.

Then, they saw it.

Just beyond a withered ridge, nestled between the roots of a monstrous, petrified tree, lay the remains of a being unlike any Isabelle had seen.

The bones shimmered faintly in the half-light fused with radiant silver and glowing fragments of crystal that pulsed with a heartbeat long gone. A halo of scorched stone surrounded the body as though the ground had once resisted holding such a being... and ultimately failed.

It was unmistakably Celestial.

Tall even in death, its ribcage opened as though it had been torn from within. Wings—yes, wings—once made of living light, now lay broken, bones like mirrored glass cracked down the centre. The skull bore no mouth, but the eye sockets burned still with threads of dormant power.

A sharp ache bloomed in Isabelle's chest as her steps faltered.

She reached instinctively for Silas, her fingers gripping the fabric of his coat tightly, anchoring herself to him as nausea rolled through her. Her breath caught. Tears gathered, unbidden.

"This... was one of me," she whispered. "They tried before."

Silas wrapped his arm around her without hesitation, pulling her into him. "You're not them," he said softly.

But Isabelle couldn't tear her eyes from the body. Its position—it had fought. One hand clutched a blade still embedded in the dirt, the other frozen mid-reach. It hadn't died on its knees. It had died standing.

Still... it had died.

"I thought I was hope," she murmured, voice trembling. "But what if I'm just... a failed second chance?"

Helena turned and walked forwards her, placing a gentle hand on Isabelle's shoulder. "Look again."

Isabelle did.

And in the pit of her soul, something shifted.

She felt her blood stir, her light responds. Not flare—deepen. As if this was not a warning, but a confirmation. The one before her had been powerful, yes. But their light had been singular, solitary.

Isabelle was different.

She wasn't just light.

She was fused—with fire, with resolve, with human fear and immortal purpose.

She wasn't born only to illuminate.

She was born to fight.

Each step forward into the Vale would not lessen her—it would forge her.

"I'm not like them," she said aloud, steadier now. "They were made to save the world. I was made to burn down whatever tries to end it."

Silas felt her pulse beneath his hand and smiled faintly. "There she is."

The Abandoned Temple

The terrain rose suddenly.

The black stone split into a jagged ravine, and from its core rose the silhouette of a temple collapsed, buried in places, but unmistakably purposeful. The air grew colder as they approached, the wind whispering through gnarled pillars and slitted arches like voices calling across time.

The temple's roof had long since fallen, allowing the grey-violet sky to spill overhead like a wound. Its walls were carved with scenes of radiant figures locked in battle with shadows glyphs that pulsed as if reacting to Isabelle's presence.

The scent was strange: scorched stone, bitter herbs, and something beneath it all—old blood and mourning. A drumbeat echoed faintly from within, though there was no drummer. Only time.

Helena knelt beside one glyph, brushing the dirt away. "This temple was a sanctuary once. A meeting ground between realms. A resting place for the protectors of the Gate."

"And now?" Silas asked.

"Now it's a tomb."

The Ghosts of the Forgotten

Then the air changed.

The fog coiled inward.

A whisper rode the wind low, guttural, layered.

And they appeared.

Figures began to emerge from the broken pillars and shadowed alcoves translucent, not quite flesh, but not spirit either. They shimmered in and out of view, glowing faintly with colours that no mortal eye had names for.

Isabelle instinctively stepped back.

But Ronan froze.

His sword dropped slightly.

His voice cracked, genuine shock, soft wonder. "It can't be..."

Three stood before them now. Familiar only in myth. But to Ronan... they were real.

"Cael," he whispered, stepping forward. "My brother."

The tallest among them golden-eyed and dark-haired, with armour etched in star-fire nodded solemnly. "I hoped you'd remember me before the end."

Next to him stood two more:

Valen – a battlemage who had once commanded the skies over the Highlands before the veil closed. His tattoos shimmered with trapped lightning, eyes sharp as broken glass.

Serael – a seer who had vanished during the Fifth Eclipse War, said to have walked into the Vale willingly to prevent prophecy from breaking.

Ronan's voice failed. He looked like a man glimpsing ghosts who had never truly died.

"You've been here... all this time?"

"Waiting," Cael replied. "Watching. The Vale is not dead—it's waiting to choose its victor. We couldn't interfere until a true light returned."

He looked at Isabelle.

"You."

Isabelle met his gaze, still holding Silas's hand. "I'm not ready," she confessed.

Serael smiled. "No one ever is. But ready or not, the storm is coming."

A howl rose from deep in the ravine far below.

Not wind. Not beast. But something sentient.

Something ancient.

The old ones were stirring.

And now... the light had arrived.

CHAPTER THIRTY-FIVE

THE LIGHT THAT REMEMBERS

The temple trembled with power not felt in centuries.

Within the broken dome, the air shimmered as Isabelle stood beneath the fractured ceiling, the shards of light and shadow cascading down upon her like falling stars. The ghosts of the past—Cael, Valen, and Serael stood in a wide arc around her, eyes glowing faintly, not with judgment but with reverence.

Each of them had fought for the light. Each had fallen into myth.

But now, they had returned to pass it on.

Isabelle's chest rose and fell with uneven breath. The power inside her felt like a storm pressing against her ribs, demanding release. She could feel the ghost-light reaching out, threading through her fingers, through her spine, her eyes, her bones.

She looked to Cael, her voice barely a whisper.

"I don't know if I'm enough."

Cael's voice was steady, calm like ocean depth. "You are more than enough. You are what we became to prepare for. You are the culmination of everything we fought to preserve."

Valen stepped forward, fingers crackling with threads of ancient runes. "We can awaken what sleeps within you but only you can shape it."

Serael added, "It's not about being ready. It's about remembering who you were before you forgot."

Isabelle's Inner Awakening

As they formed a circle around her, Isabelle closed her eyes.

The world fell silent.

And inside, she found a door.

Golden. Warm. Waiting.

She stepped through.

Suddenly, she stood in a vast expanse of stars, millions of them pulsing with life and memory. Her heartbeat in rhythm with the cosmos. She saw herself—not as she was now, but as she had once been, in another life, another war, another form. A blade of starlight in her hand. Wings of fire unfurled.

A Celestial of the Third Flame.

Born not just of light but forged in war. A protector. A destroyer of shadows.

She gasped, her eyes flying open. The golden light surged around her now, not in flickers or bursts, but in waves.

The old power had remembered her.

And she had remembered it.

Silas's Perspective

Silas stood nearby, one hand on the hilt of his sword, but his eyes never left Isabelle.

She was glowing. Not metaphorically—but truly. Her feet hovered just slightly above the stone. Her skin shimmered with silver-blue light hair swept upward as if windless fire flowed through her veins. And her eyes—those eyes he had fallen in love with burned now like celestial suns.

His breath caught.

She was no longer just the woman he loved.

She was something eternal. And he had never wanted to protect anything more in his long, weary existence.

But part of him whispered in fear—What if she becomes too much for this world? Too much for me?

He shook it off.

No.

He would rise with her or fall defending her.

Ronan's Thoughts

Ronan stared at the ritual unfolding and felt a strange emotion he hadn't tasted in hundreds of years:

Hope.

He had buried so many friends.

He had burned old dreams to ash.

And yet... watching Cael again his brother, his hero passing knowledge across the veil, watching Isabelle become, he felt a weight lift from his battle-worn shoulders.

For the first time in centuries, Ronan believed this war might be won.

But he also felt the ground beneath his feet whisper.

A different vibration.

A warning.

Helena's Fear and Resolve

Helena's heart thundered in her chest. She stood near the entrance of the temple, casting protective glyphs into the stonework, whispering incantations with her fingers trembling.

She had seen miracles before.

But this... Isabelle was becoming something sacred.

And all Helena could think was—the stronger she becomes, the more they will come for her.

She felt the shift just before it happened.

A sudden, hollow silence.

Then—a roar from deep below.

The Attack from the Depths

The ground cracked.

A gash split across the temple floor—veins of violet flame lashing out like claws. A creature burst forth from the chasm—massive, grotesque, its body a tangle of molten bone and smoking flesh. Its eyes glowed with corrupted light.

An Apex Hybrid.

The spawn of the Vale's deepest darkness.

Behind it, more creatures surged upward—misshapen beasts made of shadow and ash, limbs twisting unnaturally, mouths filled with rows of obsidian teeth.

The ghosts turned.

Cael shouted, "Defensive positions!"

Silas leapt forward, sword already flashing with celestial fire.

Ronan howled as he drew twin blades, cutting through the first beast with the precision of muscle memory and rage. "Just like old times!"

"You can say that again!" Silas shouted over the roar of combat.

Helena stood behind them, sigils crackling from her hands. "They're after Isabelle—hold them back!"

Isabelle's Light Unleashed but Isabelle was already moving, she stepped forward, arms raised.

Light poured from her, flooding the broken temple with gold, white, and deep sky-blue. Her voice rang like a bell across realms.

"I see you. I unmake you."

The Apex Hybrid snarled, lunging and was halted mid-air as her light struck it like a divine hammer, freezing its corrupted essence in a cocoon of burning starlight. Its body began to unravel, peeling back into ash.

She turned, eyes wide with power and fury, "No more will fall for me to rise."

The monsters faltered and the tide turned. The battle raged on, but something had shifted. The Vale was no longer just watching.

It was afraid and its darkest secrets had begun to tremble.

Chapter Thirty-Six

The Depth Below the Flame

T he battle had ended.

But the silence that followed was far more terrifying.

Flickering remnants of Isabelle's light clung to the temple walls like dew on cold stone, casting an eerie luminescence across the broken columns and fractured mosaics. The creatures had fallen some turned to ash, others simply dissolved into shadow, but the air remained thick with warning. This wasn't triumph.

It was only the beginning.

They stood amidst the carnage, catching their breath, blades and magic still humming in readiness. The Vale was watching them now—not as prey, but as contenders.

Each breath echoed.

Each heartbeat felt counted.

The Temple's Heart

The temple stretched deeper than they had realized.

From the main hall, broken archways led to a long corridor veined with forgotten glyphs. Mosaics of ancient battles lined the walls, much of them worn with time, depicting Celestials and monstrous forms locked in eternal combat. Their faces were blurred, but the pain carved into their bodies told stories language never could.

The scent of charred incense clung to the walls, mingled with something darker—rot, blood, old air that hadn't been touched in ages. Faint whispers seemed to slither down the corridor as they walked. They weren't loud. They were intentional—like memories trying to speak.

They walked together, weapons ready, but no one spoke. There was only the quiet thud of their boots against the stone and the soft flicker of Isabelle's residual light following them like a sentient mist.

The corridor narrowed, then opened into a circular chamber.

No door had marked it. No warning etched into the wall. It simply revealed itself as though it had been waiting for them.

The Hidden Chamber

They stepped inside.

The temperature dropped immediately. The chamber was vast but cloaked in half-shadow, walls covered in carvings too ancient to decipher. A circular dais stood at the centre, and above it—a broken dome revealing only darkness, no sky.

It was not empty.

At the far end stood a monument, a sculpted obelisk, roughly ten feet tall, made from an iridescent stone none of them had seen before. It pulsed with a slow rhythm, like a giant heart.

Upon it: words etched in flame.

Helena stepped forward, eyes wide. "It's a prophecy. And it's unfinished."

As her fingers traced the lines, they lit up, revealing text that sent a chill through them all:

"The Vale shall breathe again,

And in its breath, the fallen rise.

The blade will return to the blood it forged.

The last gatekeeper shall fall to rise no more.

The light shall burn one more time—

Or never again."

Ronan's Silence

While the others gathered around the monument, Ronan stood a few feet away.

Still. Quiet. Watching. His eyes were locked on the carving. Not in confusion... but in recognition.

His breath hitched. And then... he knew.

"The last gatekeeper shall fall to rise no more."

It was him.

He turned slightly, watching them all—Isabelle, her shoulders steady now with the weight of revelation; Silas, ever fierce, always choosing love over power; Helena, graceful in her knowledge, hands still glowing from the sigils she had carved into the air; and the ghosts Cael, his brother, Valen and Serael standing once more at the edge of the war they had never truly left.

Ronan's chest constricted with something sharper than fear.

Humility.

Not because he was lesser.

But because he had never expected to live long enough to stand among them again.

His mind wandered, unwillingly to the faces he'd once fought beside. Those who never returned. Brothers who had died screaming his name. Sisters of flame who vanished beneath the Vale's soil. Friends whose laughter still haunted his dreams.

He had walked alone for centuries not because he chose to, but because no one else had survived, so he thought.

And now?

Now he was surrounded by souls who still believed.

His fingers curled into a fist.

This is my last stand, he thought. The prophecy confirms it. I will fall. But not in vain. If I must burn, let it light their path.

Isabelle's Sensing

Isabelle turned. She had felt it—his grief, like smoke in the wind. Not fully readable. But there.

"Ronan..." she said gently.

He turned to her slowly, his face unreadable. But the pain was there, behind the stoic armour. Raw.

"I never thought I'd see him again," he murmured, glancing at Cael. "Let alone... fight beside him one more time."

"You're not done," she said. "None of us are."

His eyes flicked to hers. And in them, he saw no pity only resolve.

She believed in him.

And in that moment, for the first time in centuries, so did he.

The Shifting Air

Suddenly, the monument began to hum louder.

The glyphs around the chamber shimmered, and a soft wind swept through—though there were no openings. The whispering grew again faster this time, less like voices and more like warnings.

Helena turned toward the corridor they had come from.

"It knows we're here," she whispered.

Silas stepped forward, blade drawn. "We need to move. Whatever this chamber held back… it just told it we're coming."

Isabelle closed her eyes briefly.

And when she opened them again, her light had steadied not flaring now, not wild. Controlled. Whole.

"Then let it know we're ready."

CHAPTER THIRTY-SEVEN

THE TRIAL OF THE FORGOTTEN

The chamber pulsed once then again, harder. The air turned solid, thick with unseen force.

The glow of the monument dimmed, and the flame-etched prophecy dissolved into blackness, its final lines unreadable, as if stolen by the Vale itself.

Then the ground beneath them shifted. It didn't crack. It didn't quake. It simply... changed.

Their feet touched the same floor, but suddenly, it was not the temple anymore. It was somewhere else.

Everywhere. Nowhere. Inside them.

Silas turned sharply to Isabelle. But she was no longer at his side. He was alone.

The Vale's Trial Begins

One by one, each of them found themselves separated, standing in spaces that looked real smelled real but pulsed with illusion. Each breath they took was laced with memory, fear, and the impossible.

And overhead, like a thread pulled through all of them, a voice whispered in cruel delight:

"Two vampires... three god-like echoes of a forgotten war... a trembling witch... and a Celestial not yet fully formed."

"Such a delicious collection of failures. Yet one of you is the prize..."

"And I wonder how many will fall before she is claimed?"

It laughed then a sound like bone grinding against stone, soaked in ash and blood.

Ronan's Trial: The Last Gatekeeper

Ronan stood in a ruin. The field was soaked with blood. Moonlight glistened off swords stabbed into earth. Broken armour. Fallen friends.

He turned and there they were.

Cael.

Valen.

Serael.

But not the ones who walked beside him now, no. These were dying versions. Torn apart, faces twisted in agony. Their mouths opened in silence, mouthing accusations.

"You let us die."

"You ran."

"You survived when we needed you to bleed."

Ronan fell to his knees. His heart twisted like a rusted blade through his ribs. "I tried—I tried to save you."

"Liar."

The word rang like a war drum.

He clutched at his ears. "I didn't want to live without you!"

Then another voice cut through. Isabelle's.

"Ronan it's not real!"

The veil shimmered, and he staggered to his feet. His sword found his grip. His breath returned and the ghosts faded like smoke.

Helena's Trial: The Blood and the Bind

She stood in a small room—familiar, cozy. Books. Warm candlelight. A man's arms around her. Her lover. Long dead.

He kissed her forehead. "Stay," he whispered. "It's enough. Let them go."

The warmth was overwhelming. Her heart screamed. It had been so long since she had felt this. So long since she had been held.

"But they need me," she whispered.

"You've given enough," he replied, pressing his lips to her ear. "Be free."

Tears fell. She trembled and then she remembered Isabelle, scared and radiant, trying to hold back the dark.

"No..." she whispered.

Helena tore herself away with a scream, light bursting from her fingertips, shattering the illusion. She stood, gasping, on the temple floor once more.

Silas's Trial: The Monster Within

He stood over a blood-soaked floor, bodies strewn at his feet, Isabelle's blood on his hands.

He raised them. They trembled, he looked into a mirror and saw Lucian.

His brother's grin, wicked and cruel, stared back. His own eyes burning red, fangs slick with blood.

"You always feared it," Lucian said. "That one day you'd stop fighting the thirst. That you'd become me."

Silas stepped forward, the horror choking him, "I'll never become you."

Lucian's reflection laughed. "But you already are."

Silas closed his eyes then a memory: Isabelle's hand in his. Her kiss on his temple.

"Love will always choose you."

He opened his eyes, Lucian was gone, his reflection was his own again and he turned back to the light.

Isabelle's Trial: The Cage of Flame

She stood in a glass prison, beyond it the Vale, The temple. Her friends, screaming, dying. Silas clawing at the walls, bloodied and helpless and she—powerless.

Light tried to come, but it burned her. Her hands blistered. Her chest seared.

"You'll never be enough," the voice said. "You are the promise that fails. The light that flickers out."

She fell to her knees, sobbing, "I'm not ready."

"You don't have to be." Her own voice—but older. Stronger.

She looked up and standing before her in the reflection was... herself.

Fully formed. Wings of flame. Eyes like suns, "You only need to take the first step."

Isabelle reached up the glass shattered, and light flooded the temple.

Helena's Spell of Protection

Back in reality, Helena, her robes torn and breath heaving, raised her arms. She began drawing runes in the air, etching them into the air with blood from her own palms.

"Exoliria... mandren vasci... protectorum lucem!"

A dome of fire and moonlight erupted, anchoring all of them back into the real. The illusions fell away, the ground stopped pulsing.

The voice hissed, "You resist… but you are cracks in the same vessel. You will shatter. She will burn. And I will feast."

It laughed again long and low, a sound that hollowed the soul.

They collapsed in the centre of the chamber, exhausted and shaking, but awake.

Ronan stared at the floor, sweat glistening on his skin. He looked at each of them, Silas, Helena, Isabelle, Cael, Valen, Serael.

Still fighting. Still breathing.

And he bowed his head, not in defeat but in humility.

"You held," he whispered. "You all held."

Silas met his eyes. "We're not done yet."

Isabelle, still glowing faintly, nodded. "That was only the first trial."

Helena's fingers trembled, but her voice was firm. "Then we prepare for the next."

The chamber remained quiet, but the Vale was watching, and it would try again.

Chapter Thirty-Eight

The Breath Between Battles

The chamber was quiet now.

The oppressive presence that had cloaked them like a shroud had retreated into silence—but not absence. The Vale, wounded by their resistance, merely stepped back to observe. To wait.

Flickering firelight from Helena's protective ward pulsed gently across the temple walls. It was not quite warmth, but it was enough. Enough to keep the dark from settling too deep into their bones.

They lay in a loose circle on the temple floor some with eyes closed, others too alert to rest, but bound together in silence.

The stillness was sacred.

Healing.

The Shared Dream

It came without warning.

Not like the illusions from before, no whispers, no mocking voice. Just a gentle presence, like someone placing a hand upon their shoulders.

And then they were standing together.

Not in the temple, but in a vast void of soft starlight, suspended in nothing, surrounded by everything. The floor beneath their feet shimmered like glass stretched across a sea of stars.

Each of them looked around alert, unsure.

"Where are we?" Isabelle asked, softly.

Ronan's voice was calm. "We're dreaming. But not alone."

Cael nodded. "The Vale is sleeping… and in this breath between trials, it allowed this."

"Allowed or orchestrated?" Helena muttered warily.

But Silas stepped forward and reached out. His fingers brushed Isabelle's, and in that single contact they saw one another, not just with eyes. With memory. Emotion. Soul.

Isabelle's Reflection

They saw her first moments awakening into her power—how afraid she was to burn too brightly; how much she feared that one wrong step would destroy those she loved.

"I'm not afraid to fight," she whispered in the dream. "I'm afraid of becoming something that doesn't remember love."

Silas's hand tightened around hers. "Then I'll remind you. Every time."

Silas's Burden

They saw him holding Lucian's lifeless body after the final confrontation. Saw the nights he knelt in blood, praying to gods he didn't believe in that he wouldn't turn into the very thing he fought.

"I have killed more than I've saved," he said, quietly. "But I'll die before I let that define me."

Helena's Loneliness

They saw her study, her bookshelves covered in dust, her bed untouched for nights at a time. They saw the way she cradled memories in tea leaves and incense because they were all she had left.

"I was never meant to lead," she whispered. "I was meant to carry the map until the real saviours arrived."

Ronan stepped forward and touched her shoulder. "Then thank the stars you waited."

Ronan's Truth

And finally, they saw him alone, deep beneath the oceans of time, his blade sheathed, watching empires rise and fall. They saw the night he buried his last brother and screamed into the wind, and the day he chose not to drink blood for a year because he no longer believed he deserved to live.

"I didn't survive," he said, voice raw. "I endured."

The starlight flared and then the dream shattered.

Return to the Temple

They awoke simultaneously each gasping, each blinking away tears that had fallen during sleep. They didn't speak, they didn't need to, but the fire around them sputtered and died.

The Second Trial Begins

From the far side of the chamber, a wall shifted.

A section of stone fell away, revealing a narrow path leading downward. The air that poured from it was cold, but not in temperature in intent.

They descended together, the walls narrowed, lined with carvings that wept violet light. A hum began, pulsing in time with their heartbeats.

Then they entered a vast, circular chamber and at its centre—a creature waited, No mockery. No voice, just breathing, heavy, wet, wrong.

It was a shifting thing neither one shape nor many. Its body was slick, coated in shadows and raw sinew. From its centre, a single eye blinked open pale and filled with recognition.

They froze, the air around them thickened and then it spoke not aloud, but inside them.

"I am made from what you fear most."

"The parts of you that whisper in silence. The truths you will not say. The weaknesses you pretend are strength."

It lunged.

The Battle That Exposes

Helena tried to cast a ward, but her hands trembled, her voice cracked. The creature struck it down.

"You doubt your worth," it whispered inside her mind. "You hide behind knowledge."

Ronan's blades struck air the creature moved like smoke. "You fear dying before redemption," it hissed.

Silas slashed forward, his blade connected—but the wound turned to ash.

"You still taste your brother's blood."

Isabelle stepped forward, glowing light flaring, but the creature flinched.

It hissed. "You dare not become what you were born to be."

Isabelle gritted her teeth. "I don't have to become it," she growled. "I already am."

Light erupted It screamed, the shadows peeled back as her flame licked across its form, burning the lies. Ronan struck again, and this time his blades bit. Silas followed, blade to throat. Helena's voice steadied and flared.

Together, they pressed it back It howled as it bled starlight and smoke and finally it shattered, the chamber fell still but the silence was broken by one last whisper,

"If I am your doubt... then what waits next... is your truth."

Chapter Thirty-Nine

What the Vale Remembers

The shattered remains of the creature dissolved into the earth, its smoke curling toward the ceiling like a dying scream. But even in its defeat, it had left something behind a hollow. A lingering impression, like a bruise on the spirit. The room still pulsed with the memory of doubt.

Helena stood, hands pressed to her temples, whispering a steadying mantra under her breath. Ronan crouched near the smouldering ash, his breathing ragged, jaw clenched as he stared into the void it had left behind.

Isabelle knelt, palms against the stone floor, light still coursing through her arms. Her heart pounded not just from the battle, but from what she had felt. The way the creature had spoken into her not mocking but knowing.

It hadn't been wrong; she wasn't afraid of becoming a Celestial. She was afraid of becoming what they made her to be.

The Descent Begins

The chamber rumbled softly more a breath than a quake. A spiral staircase revealed itself at the rear wall, its steps carved from bone-white stone, lined with dim, flickering crystals that seemed to react to their movement, they descended in silence.

The deeper they went, the colder the air became not biting cold, but ancient, undisturbed. The silence here was heavy, sacred. Isabelle could feel it in her bones that something buried at the end of this descent would change everything and it did.

The Chamber of Memory

They stepped into a vast cavern.

Unlike the sharp, harsh angles of the upper temple, this place was round, soft, and organic, like the inside of a massive heart carved from the stone of the world. In the centre stood a pedestal and atop it, a sphere of radiant starlight, suspended in midair, turning slowly in silence.

Etched around the chamber walls were Celestial script, softly glowing, responding to Isabelle's presence.

As she stepped closer, the sphere flared brighter.

Her voice trembled. "This... this is a memory. Mine."

Silas placed a hand on her back gently. "From before?"

She nodded. "From before me. From when I was still becoming."

Her fingers brushed the light and then the room changed.

The Truth of Her Origin

Visions flickered across the chamber walls a battlefield. Celestial bodies burned in the sky. The Old Ones roaring. Entire cities turned to ash.

The Celestials, unable to destroy the darkness, had tried to birth a balance. Not pure light. Not just flame. But something made of earth, flesh, memory, and starlight. A being tied to the mortal realm but echoing with the divine.

They called her the Third Flame, but it had taken thousands of years.

Each attempt before her had failed. Burned too brightly. Broken too easily. Or corrupted like the one they were about to meet.

The Twisted One

A low groan echoed through the far end of the chamber, a figure stepped from the darkness, not fully man, not fully lost.

He was tall, draped in robes that were torn and fused with his own flesh. His face was mostly hidden by a cracked mask of bone and gold, but what remained beneath was warped—human eyes set in molten skin, veins glowing faintly violet. One arm had twisted into something insectile, the other limp and dragging.

Isabelle stepped back, hand glowing but Ronan stepped forward, his eyes wide. "...Marian."

The being stopped that name, a memory.

"Ronan?" the voice was gurgling, broken. "Ronan... you're still alive..."

Silas stepped protectively in front of Isabelle.

Ronan took another step. "You were my captain."

Helena's brows rose. "What?"

Ronan's voice dropped. "During the last days of the gatekeeper wars. Marian was a guardian of the final threshold. He was human. He held back the Old Ones with nothing but his sword and a prayer."

The figure laughed bitterly. "And I failed. I let them in."

"They took you," Ronan whispered.

"No," Marian rasped. "They offered. And I accepted. I thought I could control it. Gain their knowledge. Their power. Save my people."

His head tilted, revealing a jagged tear in his jawline.

"But I was wrong. And now I wait here... neither gatekeeper... nor monster. Just regret."

Isabelle's heart clenched, "You were trying to protect them," she said softly.

"But I wasn't meant to," Marian said. His gaze turned to her. "You are. You were born for it. Forged through failure. They perfected you."

She lowered her light, chest aching.

"I'm sorry." Marian's twisted form bowed slightly.

"Don't be. Just... don't waste it."

Then he turned toward Ronan, who had fallen silent, "I always knew you'd return to the threshold," Marian said, a flicker of memory in his ruined voice. "The last gatekeeper. Still holding the line."

Ronan's jaw clenched, "I would've traded places with you if I could," he said. "I would've spared you this."

Marian chuckled, a horrible, warbled sound. "You already have. You still fight. That is enough."

Then Marian stepped back into the dark and disappeared.

The Echoing Prophecy

As he vanished, the script on the chamber walls shifted, forming a new passage, bright and sharp:

"The light will rise forged from pain,

From memory made whole,

And walk between flame and shadow

To shatter what was never born."

Helena touched the wall, breathless, "It's talking about Isabelle."

Silas looked to her, and she nodded.

"I know who I am now," she whispered. "I'm the bridge. And I'm not afraid anymore."

Ronan turned to them all, "Then let's keep going," he said. "We're almost there."

But in the silence that followed, the Vale breathed again and somewhere far below, something ancient stirred awake and waiting.

Chapter Forty

The Becoming

The temple above them had faded into quiet, below, the Vale exhaled... and the world held its breath.

But for now, in the liminal breath between nightmare and dawn, they rested.

The group had made camp near the threshold to the final descent a clearing surrounded by stone pillars etched with ancient Celestial glyphs, the symbols glowing faintly in Isabelle's presence. The air was thick with magic, but just above them, the stars shimmered in a strange, purple-blue sky, like the night had cracked open to let forgotten galaxies watch over them.

A Moment Between Two Hearts

Isabelle sat near the edge of the clearing, where moonlight kissed the stone. Her golden hair glowed softly, tumbling over her shoulders as she looked out into the mist swirling below the steps. The hum of the Vale, once terrifying, now resonated in her like a second heartbeat. Her transformation had begun long before she realized it.

She didn't hear Silas approach his footsteps soundless, his presence always felt before it was seen.

He crouched beside her, his hand brushing gently over her back.

"You should rest," he said softly.

"So should you," she replied without turning.

"I can't. Not when I know what's coming."

They were silent for a moment.

Then she looked at him, her eyes full of shadowed light. "Do you remember the night you brought me tea in the library? Before all this?"

Silas smiled faintly. "You were reading about flowers that bloom in darkness. You told me you felt like one."

"I still do," she whispered. "Only now... I know I was planted in shadow so I could learn to burn."

She turned to him.

Her fingers slipped into his, and he brought her hand to his lips, kissing each knuckle as if it were holy.

"You've always burned," he murmured. "You just didn't know you were the flame."

She moved closer, pressing her forehead against his. "If I lose myself down there... if I change into something even, I can't control."

"I will remind you," he said. "Again. And again. For as long as I breathe."

Their kiss was soft at first, but then deeper, desperate not for passion, but for belonging. As if, in that one kiss, they shared every word they couldn't say, every fear they dared not name.

And when they pulled apart, her light clung to his lips. The Descent into the Heart

The next morning if it could be called morning in the Vale they stood before the final path.

The stairs were ancient, spiraling into an abyss that breathed cold fog upward like a sleeping beast. The walls tightened as they descended, the air becoming heavier with every step.

At the base was a vast cavern of obsidian, ringed with pillars taller than mountains. And at its center wrapped in chains of starlight and bone was the heart of the Vale.

There, the Old Ones stirred.

Grotesque, shifting forms, their voices like the rustling of dead leaves in a forgotten forest. They weren't just creatures—they were concepts. Fear. Despair. Lust. Greed. Hate.

They awakened.

And they saw her.

The Battle Unleashed

They moved before anyone could speak—rushing forward in unholy speed, shadows folding space.

Silas leapt, sword drawn. Ronan followed, blades glowing with blood-light. Helena began casting, hands raised high, glyphs shining from her palms.

But they were overwhelmed.

Too fast. Too many.

A claw struck Silas, sending him sprawling. A tendril wrapped around Helena's ankle, pulling her back.

And Isabelle stood still, her light flickering, the voices of the Old Ones screaming into her mind.

"You are not worthy."

"You are incomplete."

"You were made to kneel."

And Isabelle Snapped.

The Ascension

"I've had enough of this."

Her voice boomed not just from her throat, but from the core of her being. Her arms lifted as golden fire exploded from beneath her skin.

Her eyes turned to suns , her body lifted off the ground.

Her dress unravelled and reformed golden silk and stardust, cascading over her body in folds that shimmered with power. The gown left her back bare, light running along her spine like a burning constellation. The front dipped to her navel, exposing the celestial runes etched into her skin, glowing brighter with each heartbeat.

Wings erupted, Vast. Radiant. Blinding, she was no longer just Isabelle.

She was the Celestial Flame.

The Purge

The Old Ones screamed.

And she raised her hand.

"Back to the shadows you were born from."

She unleashed pure light, not just power but truth. A force that obliterated illusion and burned through falsehood. The creatures writhed, twisted, and disintegrated into shards of nothing.

Helena screamed, "The others her power will burn them too!"

She threw herself into the centre, casting a dome of protection, inscribing a sigil in the air with blood and tears, voice cracking with raw magic.

"Shield them from the divine!"

The dome flared as Isabelle's light surged filling the cavern, melting darkness, collapsing centuries of evil.

And then Silence, the light faded, smoke swirled in silence the chains at the heart of the Vale crumbled into dust.

Isabelle floated to the ground, wings folding in slowly. She looked like a goddess incarnate, her eyes no longer human but ancient, timeless, vast.

But as Silas ran to her, calling her name her knees buckled, she fell into his arms, blood on her lips and behind them a rumble. The cavern wall cracked, and a new voice echoed, deeper than anything they had heard before.

"She was never the end."

"She is only the beginning."

From the darkness, something else stirred, Older. Hungrier. Awake.